THE BUSINESS
OF NAMING THINGS

THE BUSINESS OF NAMING THINGS

MICHAEL COFFEY

BELLEVUE LITERARY PRESS
New York

First Published in the United States in 2014 by
Bellevue Literary Press, New York
FOR INFORMATION, CONTACT:

Bellevue Literary Press
NYU School of Medicine
550 First Avenue
OBV A612
New York, NY 10016

Earlier versions of the following stories appeared in these publications: "Moon Over Quabbin," *Bomb*; "Sunlight," *Conjunctions*; "Sons" and "I Thought You Were Dale," *New England Review*.

The two poems on page 200 are the work of Robert Michael Gallagher (1927–1993).

Library of Congress Cataloging-in-Publication Data
Coffey, Michael, 1954–
[Short stories. Selections]
The business of naming things / Michael Coffey. — First edition.
    pages cm
ISBN 978-1-934137-86-4 (paperback) — ISBN 978-1-934137-87-1 (ebook)
1. Psychological fiction. I. Title.
PS3553.O362A6 2015
813'.54—dc23

                                      2014025375

This is a work of fiction. Characters, events, and places (even those that are actual) are either products of the author's imagination or are used fictitiously.

Bellevue Literary Press would like to thank all its generous
donors—individuals and foundations—for their support.

Book design and composition by Mulberry Tree Press, Inc.
Manufactured in the United States of America.

FIRST EDITION

1   3   5   7   9   8   6   4   2

paperback ISBN: 978-1-934137-86-4
ebook ISBN: 978-1-934137-87-1

For Becca

What's in a name? That is what we ask ourselves in childhood when we write the name that we are told is ours.

—Stephen Dedalus

CONTENTS

THE BUSINESS
OF NAMING THINGS

Moon Over Quabbin

The woman is in Iowa now, I hear. She moved there with her husband shortly after, and now she sees. She has my eyes—a cobalt blue, opaque as marbles. She blinks them fine in my sight.

When I see the woman in Iowa, I see those eyes. They aren't mine literally; they are the eyes of my boy. I saw myself reflected in them for so many hours—thousands, could it be? My face blued, my hair orbing back, gray and wild, deeper into Matthew's irises. What would I see in those eyes in her face? I'll never know. I'll never know her.

I think of those eyes now in Iowa, in that Iowa woman's head, looking keenly over morning fields, perhaps the steam of her coffee wetting her lashes.

She has children of her own, I like to think, this woman, and of course there are problems, I can only imagine, and must. There are always problems with children, with her boy.

Not everyone has such problems as I have had, but still there are problems enough for us all, and she'll have hers even if now she can see and doesn't have that problem anymore. Most of these troubles she and her husband will surmount—the bad falls, the whooping cough scare, the man who almost talks her boy into a Greyhound bus but for the intervention of the driver, the rolled car from which he is

13

safely thrown, a fistfight in which he breaks a jaw and has an ear boxed purple. And then his jailing for possible arson, which'll bring his mother from Iowa back here to Amherst, where her boy has gone to school, at Deerfield, her blue eyes now wavering toward middle age, paler now, giving a little light, as if ice had melted in a blue drink. She will look at her shoes, waiting to see her son. And I might see him, too. His name will be Mark.

A man will come through and call her name—Mrs. White. The man is a counselor, he says, attached to the sheriff's office. He tells Mrs. White he feels her boy is innocent of any involvement in the fire. As he talks, she can only stare. He is a warm man with large features and hands. The woman bets that all his attachments are large, and she flushes with shame at such a thought at such a time. As do I.

He tells her it was a political thing—"Everything's political," she blurts out. He tells her that some kids are "after burning Amherst Hall," and she wonders at this Irish grammar; her husband would know: He's a Finnegan.

"Jeffrey Amherst," says the counselor, by way of reminding her. "The thing about the smallpox blankets?" She knows; she remembers it: the decimated Indians. He thinks to introduce himself: "I am Mr. Green."

Mrs. White can sense muscles shifting in Mr. Green's chest as he thinks and breathes and speaks. And as he listens for her.

"A political thing" is all she can say, touching again the words he has given her. A silence rings on the cold cement floor of the waiting room. The sharp clock ticks: life getting shorter.

Finally, she hugs Mr. Green. He himself has nothing more to say. Against his wide chest she can hear the deep soundings of his heart, thudding like drums in a cavern filled with water and stones. Behind it she can hear the coursing of his blood. She wants to sleep there, right there in his blood.

BEFORE MOVING TO IOWA, Mrs. White—Vera—lived in a town that is now underwater—the town of Dana, east of where I am now, maybe five miles. The state bought up four towns altogether, offering so-called market prices for homes and businesses, razing as much as they saw fit of what was left after a decent interval of looting and removal before the damming of the Quabbin River. In a year's time, the stopped river would fill the valley with water destined for the suburbs of Boston.

Mrs. White, out there in Iowa, west of Dubuque, would often imagine their basement back home, the one now solid with sludge, a small, packed room at the bottom of a vast lake; at other times it would suit her to think of their old family rec room, which her husband had built, its paneled walls and dry bar and slate pool table sitting unchanged in a cube of clear lake water—though they sold the table, that's how I see it. Along the walls the ends of large pipes visible through fractured cinder blocks like little portholes onto solid subterranean black, this the rare, strange lake with a bed of sunken sewer systems and leech fields. Often Mrs. White would think, This is an image of her mind.

Sewage and sewers and undergrounds, plumbing hidden, pipe works, many of them, going to a river bottom that's no longer a river; it's in a bigger body now. Mrs. White would be reminded of her son, who whiled away so much of his childhood in that basement, puttering alone amid his unfathomable fantasies, scheming with his friends, sneaking cigarettes and his father's girlie magazines, his mysterious, inevitable passage from bright, sweet boy to the dark station of teen-agehood transpiring there, beneath ground, and now, in her memory, under two hundred feet of reservoir water.

Her boy, Mark, had a bladder. And his mother recalled this, embarrassingly (it was in the papers), to the mother of the son—the donor—in a chance meeting at the candle factory. That is, to me. "My boy could hold an entire vat of juice before he would gush and gush for so long, his little penis would burn and the bladder itself would ache from how much it had spent," she told me. She was so devastated by the loss, the notion of parts of him carrying on as disori-enting to her as if she were in the early stages of a poisoning. She didn't know what she was saying. I had to cut her off and sit her down.

You see, I think of myself as "her" sometimes, and this is my problem. I find myself speaking of the Iowa woman as if she were myself, and vice versa. I make her come back to my town, the one underwater. I make her from here. It's all con-fused and dizzying. I find the third person more comfortable; it's easier for me to say, "Often she would think, This is an image of her mind" than to say, "Often I would think, This is an image of *my* mind," even though it is the same thing. Perhaps it has to do with upbringing. I was always able to tell my son that he was as good as anyone else, that he could be anything he wanted, whereas I could not say the same to myself, or say that of myself to others. Or even complain.

But it is I who thinks often of the Quabbin Reservoir, since we lost Matthew—our vacation in Italy, roadside bandits, a gunshot, his forehead. I see myself walking along the reservoir bottom, what we returned to, and there meeting the ghosts of the four communities, walking—more like wading—from town to town, up the long hill to Enfield, now a dark, weedy

mound alive with bubbles and spiked with stalking muskel-
lunge, or whatever, maybe pike—my husband would know;
over to Greenwich, where the Jackson barn still wavers erect,
and on to Prescott, where I wrecked our car on a culvert I still
don't see. It's lonely down here, but somehow peaceful. Of
course there's an absence of life, but then again, proof that
there has been life. Between the towns of Enfield and Dana,
on my way home, near an old wagon upended and headed
for the water's surface but for the wagon tongue sunk in silt, I
see that woman whose eyes are my son's, are mine. "What are
you doing underwater?" I ask, and she rises, out of sight in a
shaft of captured air and light, to the surface.

I HAVE TRIED TO MAKE SOMETHING, anything at all, of my
boy's passing. I have told his life story to myself, over and over,
starting from his conception on Pequod Hill one gorgeous
May dawn, through his early troubles with his feet, to his
Little League triumphs and his father's pride and the first girlfriend—and his father's fears!—and all the rest, those teenage
years, right up to the shooting, and nothing coheres. But it's
not only my boy's story that doesn't come together but everything else as well—my own story, my life as a mother, my
parents', or my sister's life, or the life as I know it of June, my
neighbor, and of anyone else I know who is not famous (their
lives always seem to come together, don't they?).

What I can grasp is what is left of him—his eyes in the
Iowa woman's head, his heart in the chest of the man from
Amherst, his kidneys in that boy from the valley, whose name
I know. I imagine they'll all meet sometime. I imagine I'll
meet them all myself, too, in time, but as I say, I just imagine
it. But when the moon is full and bright in the sky, that one

moon that is everyone's moon, I know it tugs on the tides of my boy, his humors, wherever they are. And as they lean together, in one direction to its pull, like the weeds under Quabbin, leaning, I know that each is aware of the other, of itself, of their original self. And as they move toward the light, wherever they are, at times like this I know the moon, and the water, and what it all means.

THE BUSINESS OF
NAMING THINGS

———

H E WAS IN THE BUSINESS OF NAMING THINGS, like Adam.

William Claimer was very happy with this thought, which he formulated for himself on his forty-eighth birthday as he sat alone on the main concourse at Penn Station, waiting for a train. The molded chair he sat in, plastic and orange, held him like a hand. Claimer thought back: He'd been naming things for twenty-five years.

He could remember the first thing he'd ever named—his daughter, Elise. He loved the name, first of all—its sound; and he loved elision and the *g* missing from the French word for *church*. He had envisioned for his daughter a life of gentle winnowing, a life made by defining and excluding what one was not. All that in the absent *g*.

Actually, Elise was doing well now—she was at the Sorbonne. In a recent aerogramme she declared, with an acquired Gallic arrogance, that she believed in a kind of God that had no faith, an "atheosophy," she called it. Pall, two years her junior and Claimer's only other child, was an early onamastic mistake (onamastics: the practice or science of naming). The idea was to refer to him as "Paul"; that is, to pronounce it like the fine saint's name but to give in the spelling another option—a choice of sober introspection over piety, perhaps. But Pall from the very beginning refused a demeanor of dignified pall, and his friends, influenced by a trademark that the usually diligent Claimer had overlooked, began to call him "Mall," a further nicking on the nickname Pall Mall, after the cigarette. Pall grew up sullen and harsh. At the moment, he was in jail. A pall of the wrong kind.

TRADEMARKING WAS THE NAME of Claimer's game, and he'd made a fortune at it. He'd begun in advertising, brighter than bright, top of his class everywhere—public school, prep school, college, college. An M.Phil. from University College, Dublin, a specialty in Hopkins. *Wolfsnow* was from Hopkins.

When the Seagram's account came forth with a new product—a frozen cranberry mix for vodka—he thought, Wolfsnow. They bought it, and how. Right down to the logo, a white wolf standing in the snow, a vague kill beneath its paws and the suggestion of droppings of blood. If it had been a grapefruit mix, inevitably a piss-pale yellow, Wolfsnow would not have done, would it? But then he wouldn't have thought of it.

Wolfsnow entered the vocabulary of mixology and Claimer became a partner.

He took over all the "vice" accounts—Seagram's, Liggett & Myers, a microbrewery. For a while, most of Claimer's duties fell to the spending of client money on campaigns long under way, but the firm soon was abuzz with the task of naming another new product—a nonalcoholic beer from Bard & Co., whose line of Bard lagers and ales was legendary in the

Northeast. Claimer came up with Innisfree, more poetic lar-
ceny, but his little world raved.

Ten years ago, Claimer packed up his peculiar genius and
went on his own. He cribbed a paper from an obscure journal
of onamastics dealing with the etymology of the naming of
American towns, and sent the text to the most prominent
journal in the building trades.

It was the eighties, and condominium communities
were going up all over New England. Hillock Green, outside of Springfield, Arbor Grove in Bennington, Cedar Dale,
between Northampton and Amherst, Pine Ridge in Southport, all were his. Easy money, forty to a hundred thousand
per, depending on the size and price range of the development. Once he had established himself as an expert, all it
required was a look at local history and a sensitivity to setting.
And a good investment portfolio.

Claimer wasn't the only man in his field, of course, and he
monitored his colleagues closely. He delighted in the Ohio
fellow who came up with the two horn blasts in "Double
A [honk-honk], M-C-O." He admired the proprietary spirit
of Robert Young gently insisting that it was "Sanka brand
decaffeinated" coffee, to avoid the horror of all trademark-
ers—that a product name become a generic reference, like
Kleenex. And he felt a little thrill when a naming went awry,
like "Infiniti," which, despite his own highly trained ear and
eye he always pronounced "Infin-EE-ty," as if the $45,000
luxury car were a diminutive form of *infin*, whatever that is.
Ah, well. The fellow from Long Island shouldn't feel too bad:
When Chevy's Nova was introduced into the Mexican market,
the manufacturers suffered to realize it meant "won't go" in
Spanish. Born loser, as the Chicanos would say.

Speaking of fate: Claimer didn't believe much in it. In

fact, he didn't believe in it at all. But what other word could explain buying salmon at the fish market that was wrapped in an out-of-town newspaper that contained a story about a community's decision to change the name he had given it? Perhaps *fate* is too common a word, but there is no explaining this, as there is no explaining why his wife did not come home for his birthday dinner that night. So he ate the two salmon steaks and composed a note to Clare, saying that he was getting out of town for a few days. He would leave the next morning.

HE STOOD OUTSIDE PENN STATION and smoked a joint. He still smoked joints. It was his single vice. It kept him young, he felt. He'd only resumed the pot habit—and it wasn't really a habit—around the time he began to jog, to reduce a slight paunch. He had Pearl Jam and Arrested Development and a few other hot bands in his tape carousel at his office. He liked to hew to a younger rhythm.

It was pleasing to feel connected to today's youth, and it felt less dangerous. Reading about Ice-T in the *Journal* did a funny trick. And he couldn't help notice that the high end of today's consumer culture wanted him to feel connected and safe, accepted. The new bodies: Not buxom and buffed as in his courting days (which would make him feel old, wouldn't it, and desperate), but lean, hard, waifish models like that Kate Moss of the Calvin Klein ads with her hands in Markey Mark's pants, or standing by herself, holding her own feeble breast. She wanted a meal from a man with means, a man with silk boxers.

It was irrational to be seduced by this nonsense, to be swayed and persuaded. After all, Claimer had spent two dozen

years being faithful to Clare. He drove a Volvo. He even had
a gun. And yet, here he was, feeling something beginning to
loosen. He felt himself edging toward an indiscretion, a fault
line, however dangerous.

There were ten minutes until the train, so Claimer decided
to grab a coffee before boarding. A woman who'd eyed him
twice already walked over to him. She was spectacularly freckled. The close-set orange dot work on her forehead looked like
an enlargement of orange lithography. Her eyes were green.

She said, "Are you Henry?" obviously there to meet someone she'd never met before. There was a loveliness to her that
the wild smatter of her skin made unreachable, like a child
disappearing in a pointillist landscape. She looked about thirty.

Even though it was November, she was in short sleeves.
Her arms carried an even finer dot than her face, the orange
approaching salmon. She seemed otherworldly, from another
planet or species.

Claimer said "No" to her question, before thinking about
it. He might have said "Yes."

She immediately turned, sharp on one toe—she had heels
on. Her dress was a green pinafore and her legs were stock-
inged white. Her figure was as narrow as an ironing board.

She strode back to an older balding man with square tinted
glasses, like the ones Ari Onassis wore. He looked evenly at
Claimer over the woman's shoulder. Her hair was a brassy yellow and hung straight down her back, ending at the middle
of her small ass like a perfect broom. The man said something
to her, and the two of them moved on.

Later, sipping the coffee that tasted as if two cubes of cardboard had been dissolved in it, he saw them again. Claimer
was on the main floor, cupped in his seat. He could see them
milling about at the top of the escalator, looking for Henry.

Claimer was tempted to do it, claim he was just checking them out, that he really was Henry, and take it from there. These are the kinds of things people do in stories—they walk up and become another person just to see where it will take them. Claimer liked that, the abandon of it, and wished it for himself. That's when he realized what he was: in the business of naming things. Like Adam.

GOING THROUGH OSSINING, Claimer took note of a few trackside haunts visible from the train. He imagined them to once have been frequented by John Cheever, who used to live in a big house up from the river. The yacht club, with a bar; the boatyard filled with cabin cruisers in dry dock, in one of which Cheever would have drinks with a friend and never sail, but instead conjure deck-rail views of the wisping spumes of the sea, and quote Conrad; along the track bed the late asters riffling. Cheever would have noted them, too.

Above Ossining, after the prison with its gray walls topped by a mad scribble of razor wire, north and across the river, a white gull settled in the middle of a landfill covered with black plastic, gentle as a thought. Claimer kept it in his mind's eye for miles.

THE MAN SEATED NEXT TO HIM was a linguist at Bard. Claimer had met him once at an MLA symposium on the Latinate in Hopkins, but he'd forgotten the fellow's name. Claimer struck up a conversation anyway. His field of inquiry was the structural analysis of the infinitive *to seem*. When Claimer asked him how he'd ever come to have such a specialty in life—for Claimer, a specialist himself, was always interested in precise choices in a world of unreason—the man said he didn't know.

Claimer asked him if he knew the Wallace Stevens poem that ends "let be be finale of seem."

The man said he'd read it as a student. He even remembered the title, "The Emperor of Ice-Cream." "Perhaps that's what did it," he said, returning to his PowerBook.

"Did what?" asked Claimer.

There was no reply.

"What do you think of Saussure?" ventured Claimer. He opened his own PowerBook to signal his agreement that work, not idle chatter, was the primary interest. He called up LING, his dictionary of linguistic terms (he had several of the Penguin category lexicons—math, music, geology, botany—on his hard drive).

"He was skeptical too early, like Nietzsche," said the linguist, who introduced himself—Alston Remard—and proffered a hand. "They both were just guessing."

"The word is a sign made up of signified and signifier," recited Claimer. He then gave his own name. "And the relationship of signifier to signified is totally arbitrary. What do you think of that?"

"Gobbledygook," remarked Remard with a broad smile. A homely man, thought Claimer. His face, in repose, was pitched in a kind of dignified gloom. But when grinning, he looked crazed and dim.

"You're wrong," said Claimer, smiling back but then quitting it. "People will believe anything. Joes become Joes, when they should be Jims. Morgan—Morgan?—becomes Morgan, well, somehow. People even say in-FIN-ity for that car, for crissakes."

"I own one," said Remard. "What do *you* call it?"

"Forget it," said Claimer.

Claimer tried another tack, for the sport of it, but the linguist didn't want to talk about whether the unconscious was structured like a language. And Rhinecliff, the Bard College stop, was next. As the homely little linguist trundled off toward the end of the car, Claimer thought to himself, If a playwright and a beer and a college can all be called Bard, who's right then anyway, asshole?

North of Albany, Claimer found himself becoming fatigued. Middle age, which Claimer would only concede was approaching, had a smaller tank. As the track cut through the umber fields between Saratoga and Whitehall, he found himself having such profound thoughts as: Are the smarter cows the ones who seem to notice the train and look up, or the ones who remember seeing the train every day and don't?

In the bottomland between two fields of browned clover ran a dark vein. The Scottish call it "a burn." It fell drippingly into the wide, calm heart of Lake Champlain. Claimer fell asleep for a while.

IT WAS ONE OF HIS FAVORITES, Jump Hill; perhaps because it was in the Adirondacks, where he'd grown up; or perhaps because he took possession of a unit there in return for his naming the community. It was a small two-bedroom just off the management office and groundskeeper's shed.

Jump Hill, the name, had come easily to him. The twenty-six-unit development was built on a hill west of Lake Placid, with a view of the ninety- and seventy-meter ski jumps. It was a name simple, modest, and light—it sounded like a childhood nickname for a favorite sledding slope. The community was eight years old now and it wanted to change its name. The nerve.

The article Claimer'd found darkening around his fish was from a Providence weekly, credited to the Scripps-Howard news service. It looked like a little space filler on a page otherwise full of menus and housecleaning tips. Claimer took it out of his briefcase and read it:

What's in a Name?

"We have nothing against Olympic sports, and we are proud of the Olympic tradition in this area," said Kallie Ford to a roomful of fellow condo owners at Jump Hill, near Lake Placid, N.Y. "We just wish to acknowledge what we feel is a more significant legacy of the land on which we dwell—I now christen our home, our development, Timbucto."

By unanimous vote of the 26 shareholding parties at the 8-year-old cedar-shingle development set high upon a hill in New York's Essex County, about 100 miles northwest of Albany, a small community's name was thus changed. Jump Hill, the name by which the community had been known since before ground was broken, is a reference to the two Olympic ski jumps visible on a mound to the east of the property. Buyers of the one-, two-, and three-bedroom units, which were originally priced in the $40,000–$85,000 range, had no choice in the original naming of the community. There is considerable dispute in the region as to whether another bid for an upcoming Winter Olympics should be made, and to what purpose the ski jumps stand.

Ms. Ford, before calling for the show of hands voting the new name, reminded the assembled

property owners that the original name was the cre-
ation of "a paid consultant who never came here
and never will. He just took a check." [Claimer
would be pleased to remind Ms. Kallie Ford that
he did not receive a check for naming Jump Hill,
that he was indeed a bona fide shareholder and
that he was not informed of the vote, as called for
in the bylaws. Not unanimous.] *Timbucto* [the
article concluded] *was the name of a short-lived*
settlement of free blacks in the 19th century.

This was nothing Claimer'd run across in his research,
though admittedly he'd done rather little of it for this job,
since he was a native of the area and felt he knew the history
and terrain well enough to fulfill his duties. But it had been
eight or nine years, probably ten, since he'd done the actual
work. He checked on his PowerBook. A few summers ago,
before the incarceration, he'd paid his son ten dollars an
hour to input notes from his case files.

He searched for "Jump" and found the file:

1984. Fessette & Doe Bldrs. Justnow Corp. Chitten-
den Bank (Burlington, Vt.). 1, 2, 3. 26U. Olympic
site, '32, '80. U.S. beat USSR. Craig & Dad.

I remember that [This must be Pall, on a stoned
riff, Claimer thought]. The big triumph over the
Russians, what an upset, the gold medal, and
weren't the hostages being held? And the goalie
named Jim Craig, all sweaty still in his pads skating through the pandemonium on the ice, guys
raising their sticks & hugging & falling down,
the crowd going nuts, & this goalie who'd played

great looking for his father in the crowd & you
could see his mouth going Where's my Dad?
Where's my Dad? with a pained look on his face.

Claimer was touched by this. Jesus, we always hurt our
children. The text went on:

Bucker & I broke into the Field House one night.
The ice was still up & the rink was dark except for
the surface itself, which had a pale glow. We took
turns sliding on our shoes from in front of the
crease, zigging & zagging back & forth over to
the boards, shouting Where's my Dad? Where's
my Dad? Laughing hysterically. Bucker's Dad
was some drunk who'd moved back to Texas &
mine—Dear Dad, are you reading this? Oh, you
were a good guy all right. I'm still laughing.

Pall was a handsome boy. He looked like that actor Johnny
Depp. That is to say, he had soulful eyes, ratty hair, and a
theatrical pout. The boy was a mistake, as Claimer's generation called births that occurred despite Copper-7's and
diaphragms and the Pill. Pall's early childhood hyperkinesis
was, as the Claimers had hoped, only a stage, but unfortu-
nately one that gave way to a profound indolence. The kid
sleep-walked his way through the Dalton School and a year
at Oberlin, to which he said good-bye, apparently without
having cracked a book.

Claimer insisted that the boy reenroll somewhere, and Pall
announced that he was headed for Paul Smith's College, a
school specializing in forestry up near Saranac Lake. It had
some other specialties, too.

"What do you know about it?" asked the father, a little guiltily.

"It's a party school, Dad."

At least it's not because of the Paul, reasoned Claimer to himself.

So Pall holed up in the Jump Hill condo, which wasn't far from the campus, for two years, doing God knows what. He left school again, in the spring of '87, and was arrested with five pounds of dope while heading into Canada.

Claimer's lawyers were hopeless in the Quebec courts, and Pall was serving a harsh eight-to-twelve-year sentence at St. Vincent de Paul (again!) prison outside of Montreal.

Claimer had plans to visit his son once he'd checked out the Jump Hill—or rather, Timbucto—situation. He was more curious than anything; he couldn't have cared less that the name had been changed, nor was he really miffed about not being notified of the vote. After all, as the little article said, what's in a name?

Claimer hadn't been upstate in several years—during Pall's trial, and the painful visits to St. Vincent de Paul's, he'd gone straight to Montreal by plane, skipping altogether the North Country. The last time Claimer'd actually been to northern New York State was when he opened the condo one winter— it was '89 or so—to see if he really wanted to rent it out, now that Pall had vacated for other accommodations to the north. He and Clare had stayed at Mirror Lake Inn. All he could remember was that they had some good lovemaking in the snow-silenced dawn. The good old days.

The train trip dragged on. Perhaps it was the teenage rowdiness up at the front of the car that prolonged the journey. His son's kind of people, a mixed group of eight encamped at one end, the boys, their big boots braced on the seats, swilling

Molson and loudly crunching potato chips, empty cardboard trays skating about underneath the seats, the girls a bit more demure, peeling fruit, chewing gum. One was particularly pretty; she had a little bobbed hairdo like that figure skater Dorothy Hamill. She talked incessantly in a soft voice while the boys gamboled about and the other girls looked at the boys. She flipped her hair in the middle of every sentence and said "but like."

But when Claimer heard her say something about "my grandmother's ex-boyfriend," he felt a wave of affection for this child, out in a world that was already brutalized for her in a way that was all too easy to comprehend: Love didn't last. He felt flushed with pride that he and Clare were still together—at least technically.

The station call for Plattsburgh finally came, and Claimer had to endure several minutes of raucous celebration from the Kiddie Korner, as if they were the ones who'd suffered the journey most. He wondered just what forms of revelry awaited them beyond the train. Cartwheels?

The rental car—gray under a gray sky, a Ford of some sort—sat next to the little depot, keys in it, as the agent had promised. The trusting North Country. In the rearview mirror he did see one of the lads do a standing backflip, like Ozzie Smith.

Claimer made his way out of Plattsburgh; he knew the way from years past. He took the new—not new, it had to be twenty years old by now—expressway, headed west toward Placid. The sky was getting leaden, clouds indistinguishable from one another. It looked like snow.

It was almost winter, and not even Election Day yet. A Montreal deejay announced, "Wouldn't it be nice if it were aboot twenty-five degrees oot and the sun was shining."

The clocks had just been turned back, and dark came early. Snow started spitting around Oreville and quickly thickened. The headlights penetrated through cones of dashing white flakes that drew the eye inward, calling for a certain steely caution.

By the time he got to Mirror Lake Inn, the trees were cuffed in snow. The inn sat above the lake like a cathedral, inviting and warm, lighted as if by jewels.

After a soothing scotch at the bar, Claimer settled in to his room and then retired. He fell asleep immediately, a colorful tumble of mental imagery dropping him nicely to the floor of unconsciousness like an anchor. He called his wife first thing in the morning, but she was either still asleep or out. Or still out? He read through the room menu—lots of game on it— and he fingered the Gideon's Bible, reminding himself of the names of the Gospels. But Clare didn't call, so down he went to his "Adirondack breakfast."

He said hello to Jack Trudeau, who was having coffee with a few men in the bright dining room that overlooked Mirror Lake, stolid and black with cold but still open. Jack was Garry's father. Claimer'd met him at Garry and Jane's house on the Sound a year or so ago in the course of doing the Southport job. He couldn't remember if Jack had a piece of the inn or not.

"What's this about Jump Hill?" he asked Jack—a handsome gray-haired man with a fast smile.

"Don't know, Bill. The return of John Brown? I don't know."

The conversation deteriorated into introductions and then moved on quickly to "Nice to meet you" and "Say hello to Garry and Jane" before any more detail on Timbucto was possible. Claimer sat over his decaf and muffins—he passed on the venison sausage and duck eggs—trying to remember John Brown.

Claimer called ahead and spoke directly with Ms. Kallie Ford. She answered, "Timbucto. Can I help you?" somewhat embarrassed at the rhyme. You could tell the greeting was still new in her mouth.

Reading from the deed, he explained to her that he was the shareholder in unit 3 and was in Placid on business and was planning to stop by later in the morning. She laughed like a sparrow being freed. It was quick and disappearing.

"We look forward to seeing you then," she said.

As he drove through the streets of Lake Placid, the snow squeaked and crunched beneath the tires like Styrofoam. Claimer wondered what advantage was smuggled in Ms. Ford's voice. He'd noted the "we" as well.

The upstate environs had not really changed much over the years. When Claimer was a boy, there was Plattsburgh, the only genuine city north of Glens Falls, with traffic lights and Canadians and an air force base, and politicians dressed in suits. And it was probably still the only place in the whole of the Adirondacks with a gay bar and a Chinese restaurant. The rest of the area was poor, a lapsed rural economy given over to a corrections industry and truck repair. All the officeholders from the surrounding little towns wore plaid shirts in their election posters. You could still see them posted in the stores and on telephone poles. Placid and Saranac Lake had a bit of shine, by virtue of the winter Olympics of 1980. Some new structures thrown up, and some fancy stores; a Hilton. But it couldn't hide the long-term effects of tough winters on the architecture, not to mention the people. Claimer's wife had once called them "wolfen."

Still, Claimer was moved by things that would not change. He admired them. It's what made him a Republican. In immutability Claimer sensed a certain godliness, a peculiar mix of faith and fear that kept things stable. And he could feel it here, in the North Country. There were even scarecrows in the fields.

The ski jumps came into view like two Chinese ideograms sketched on a surface of white, each a thin rising stroke that plummeted, dark and thick, to the ground. High up on the hill, he could see the clutter of cedar homes and cars parked obliquely to some design. This was Timbucto.

Claimer despaired for a moment at the loss of Jump Hill. It was exactly right—the eye was led, as he had just been reminded, from the jumps up the hill. Even the spondaic meter of the name Jump Hill conveyed a stepping up. Too, too bad.

The new name was burned into a wooden sign hanging by chains from a deep post. There was an ugly stone trough, as big as a bus, set off behind the tree, as if for the feeding of some Yeti. A sculpture, no doubt. Ah well . . .

When Claimer parked the car in the lot in front of the management office—the sign said COMMUNAL CENTER—there was a man standing in the walk, his face unseeable within the tunnel of the fur-edged hood. He greeted Claimer with an extended right hand and Claimer saw that it was his son.

He repressed the urge to ask him if he'd escaped. "Pall," he said.

"River Phoenix died last night," his son said vacantly. "We're all a little fucked-up—worked up—about it here, you know. Like, you can't believe it."

Like, I can, thought Claimer, but he said, "Who?"

Pall took his father's bag and headed up the walk.

"You know, Dad," said Pall as they reached the door to the communal center. "You used to mock the guy. The name is

Phoenix. River Phoenix. Some James Bond thing you'd do, remember?"

Claimer did remember. Pall had had a picture of the young actor on his wall—a poster from a Rob Reiner film. Claimer couldn't get over the audacity of naming yourself—or perhaps some agent had done it—after a body of water and a city.

"You always said that River was no name for an older man. He'd regret it someday, you said. People'd call him 'Old Man Ribber.'"

"Gee, son, I don't know what to say."

"It was his real name, you know."

Before taking in the high stone and wood interior of the room—an A-frame-type chalet—Claimer had to ask, and he did in a whisper: "What are you doing here? I was set to visit you tomorrow."

"Oh, real sorry, Dad, sorry to disappoint you," Pall said sarcastically.

A tense pause. Claimer scanned again the vertical space he was in; he noticed a banner, hanging behind the main counter, which said AESTHETIC DEMOCRACY.

"Work release. Kallie—Kallie Ford—arranged it. Can I call you Bill?"

"Sure, son."

"Call me PM. We've done away with the relational around here, okay?"

"Sure. PM."

He saw the brassy hair; it swung once like a narrow curtain on the other side of the desk and from behind it the orange bone of her shoulder turned. And then the livid face. It was her all right.

Claimer clomped toward the desk. Her green eyes in the brilliantly speckled composition of her face reminded him of something—something homey and familiar. And faintly distasteful. He tried to elude it before it settled on him: peas and carrots.

"William Claimer, welcome to Timbucto. We are pleased to have you. PM has told us much about you and now we get to see you with our own eyes."

For some reason, her words cadenced into a spectral poetry in Claimer's ear. "I'm Kallie Ford," she said, extending a hand with skin as dark as a toad's. Her fingers were cool. Claimer found nothing to say, and he felt it.

"I could have been Henry," he blurted out.

Her left eye closed a bit, in a kind of comic discernment. He let her think. A moment passed, and he could hear his son shuffling nervously behind him. Was there something between them?

"You still can be," she said. "As you know, we renamed ourselves here. We do it all the time."

PM hustled his father off through a side door. "It's a bit shabby, Dad. *Bill.* Hard habit. But the sheets are clean."

Claimer hurled over his shoulder to Ms. Ford, "We'll talk about New York. Penn Station? Yesterday morning?" It was too jolly, he feared. Still, she smiled.

PM gave Claimer the rundown, sounding as if he'd rehearsed it. "Six months of this and I'm free. I work with the community here, but it's really based in Canada, through Kallie. I'm doing drug counseling." Other details came forth about PM's plans as he hurried to anticipate and satisfy the usual fatherlies. But Fatherly was aswirl with the gentle ringings of Ms. Ford's voice and her freckled beauty.

"She's in charge," said PM, reading in the opaque revolutions of his father's attentions something he recognized as hunger or want, like when he would suddenly look up from his newspaper and scan the kitchen ceiling.

"I have to talk to her about this Timbucto thing," Claimer said weakly.

PM offered his view. "It's like this, Bill. They mean no disrespect. It's just that, well, here things are done a little different. People understand the past here. And how it can be used for the future, I guess. You know, did you see that banner out there? Here, it's on this stationery here: Aesthetic Democracy. We vote on everything, and the main thing is what's most artful, you know, like pleasing. Like we're considering a new accent. For everybody. The best spoken English. Wessex or something. And we'll all learn it."

Claimer said, "Just tell me this, and I'll drop it. What is Timbucto? I looked in my files—you remember?—and there was nothing on it but your little ice capade, 'Where's my dad?' thing."

"Okay, Dad. Fuck it! John Brown, the abolitionist. Harpers Ferry? Wanted to attract runaway slaves and set up a free state up here, for black people. They called it Timbucto. Never went anywhere. But it was a beautiful idea, and that's why we voted it in."

Not bad, thought Claimer.

THE YOUTH OF TIMBUCTO, led by PM, it turned out, had pressed for a midnight vigil for the late Mr. Phoenix. PM worked as industriously as a UAW organizer all afternoon—first on the phone in the kitchen and then speeding to other units to make face-to-face appeals. A quorum was rounded up for the 8:00 P.M. vote. Claimer begged off, claiming that he had to listen to *Marketplace* on the local public radio station, but he slipped in the side of the Communal Center at about 8:15. His son had the floor, dark hair brushed back, his face daggered in shadow. He looked amazingly famous, better than an actor. He looked like the young Artaud. Claimer, with a dad's pride, felt there were women and girls swooning as Pall shyly swayed back and forth, his index finger pressed thoughtfully to his lower lip, as he searched for the right words. He broke into a little speech that was obviously memorized from one of the dead actor's parts. A few of the girls and some teenage boys cheered at the end. PM seemed exhausted by the effort; his dark clothes hung loose upon him, as if he had just suddenly lost weight. With nothing left to say, he looked like he would collapse with indecision—should he sit down?—when Ms. Kallie Ford came forth and put an arm around his waist and called for a vote. "Let us hear your voice," she said, while looking through PM's hanging forelock for his eyes.

It was unanimous; the adults took evident joy in giving their sons and daughters—their coequals in this high-minded community—the right to a ritual they wanted. Ms. Ford and Claimer's son hugged.

Claimer went up to Kallie Ford when the meeting was over. He quickly explained that he had come to Timbucto to investigate the name change—did she know that he had done the original incorporated ID?; she did. But that it really didn't bother him? It didn't. He was now here to see his son. During his little confession, Ms. Ford had been tending to a string of people who needed to have some small thing or another acknowledged, a task she handled with effortless charm. But when he mentioned seeing his son as his current priority, she squared her body and appraised him in a schoolmarmish way, a silent admonition. She knew it was a lie.

"Will you come over for a drink," he said. And she did.

"WE ARE VERY FRANK HERE, Mr. Claimer. I have many lovers."

Claimer, oddly, was not taken aback. She was in his house, his unit 3, after all; and it was late. Well, ten o'clock. And they were alone.

"I didn't intend to pry," said Claimer, "about your many lovers."

"It could not be prying, could it?" she said, swirling the scotch in her glass. "I told you."

She sat on the hassock in Claimer's open living room. Her loose peasant blouse disguised the secrets of her breasts.

"Where are you from?" he asked. Claimer could have been dressed a little more sportily. He had on gray woolen slacks with a sharp crease and a cotton turtleneck. His loafers struck him as terribly square. "Do you want to smoke some grass?"

She laughed an assassinating laugh, and said no thank you, noncommittal as to whether she ever indulged, though she was working her drink with a veteran's verve.

"I'm an artist," she said. "I work with stone and steel. I'm from Canada."

Claimer mentioned the one sculpture exhibit he had seen—the work of Anthony Caro—and the trip he'd made to Storm King.

"My, my," said Kallie Ford, draining her drink while laughing in it.

She moved forward on the hassock, a signal that she was leaving. Claimer scrambled. "Is that your work, on the drive coming in?"

"Yes," she said, settling back for a minute and taking an ice cube into her mouth. "Do you like it?"

Claimer actually had an opinion. "It's marble, is it?" he guessed.

She nodded, as if this was a common mistake. "No. Limestone." She brightly chewed her ice.

She's playing, thought Claimer. She thinks I'm a fool. Well, so then: "What the hell is it?"

"It's a word. A word in the stone. *Ocean.* There's a word in every stone."

Then she was standing, holding out her glass for him to take. "You should come to the vigil tonight. There will be a movie." She canted her head to the side. This was a bribe. "C'mon. It won't be that heavy. The kids just want to feel good about this friend they feel they've lost. He was a very gifted actor, you know. And a beautiful boy."

"I just may do that," said Claimer, wanting to be a beautiful boy. "Ocean. I'll have to take another look."

CLAIMER DID GO DOWN FOR THE VIGIL. It was held right where the vote had been held, in the Communal Center. The mood was both festive and funereal; people milled about, the kids dressed in black, munching from cups of popcorn. There was a crudely painted banner hanging beneath the Aesthetic Democracy one, reading RIVER: 1970–1993.

The lights went down and everyone sat. No ceremony at all. On a large-screen TV, the FBI warning sat and stayed. "Hit fast forward," said someone, and the image went into the fibrillation that meant it was speeding by. Whoever had the remote also raced through some coming attractions for movies no doubt already come and gone and now on video; Claimer recognized Emma Thompson, who was telling some joke and flipping her hair and closing a door. And then a road scene and time seemed to stop: the film.

Several of the kids, and then more, chanted along with the voice-over narration. "I always know where I am by the way the road looks. Like I just know that I've been here before . . ."

What's this? thought Claimer. Ah, well. The sensation of profundity. So the kids are alright.

Claimer looked for his son and spotted him. In the front row, arm in arm in arm with about five other kids in a chain. No call for a father there. Kallie Ford was not in evidence. In fact, Claimer realized he might be the only bona fide adult left in the place, now that he looked around. Where had the others his own age gone to? His own age? My God, he thought, it's after midnight. And then sleep took him.

"I just want to kiss you, man." A man's voice. Claimer was rubbing his eyes, awake. On the screen, two guys were sitting around a campfire. Later, his wife entered his twilight imagery as he drifted again. They had an argument. They were throwing plastic champagne glasses. Things escalated into passion. Clare was saying *glass* and *ass* as if there were some mystical linkage between them that suggested human linkages. They wrestled on the bed and then went still. Clare slowly worked the stem of the champagne glass up his ass. And she said, "There." Claimer could see Kallie Ford in the corner of what had been his old office, her freckled face peeking out from behind a curtain.

Claimer woke up in the empty Communal Center. It was dark. He let himself out the side door and made his way to his unit. All the lights there were still on, but this son wasn't in his room, or anywhere. Claimer turned the lights out and headed for bed. It was 3:00 A.M. He noticed a brightness out behind his place. He saw the roiling silver of a Jacuzzi, scarves of white steam lifting into the dark. He'd not seen it before—a big redwood deck and a sloshing tub. They must have added it since he was last here, he realized. He saw a thin bare back at the far edge turn toward him. It was Kallie Ford. She held handfuls of smoking snow. She stood there in the churning water, rubbing up the length of her arms and across and down the declivities of her chest. The red ran off of her like blood.

Wolfsnow, thought Claimer, fondly for an old idea.

He watched for a long time. It was a transformation he could not credit or understand. Nor did he want to, somehow. It was enough just as it was.

He tried with his eyes to search the caul of darkness. He looked for his son to materialize, or for some "Henry" to appear. He could almost envision his own figure lurking at the lip of the Jacuzzi, admiring at closer range the luminous pearling of Kallie Ford's body. But he would not move.

In the end, he went to the kitchenette and made a cup of tea. He called his wife but hung up after two rings: he'd drawn a blank on her name.

SUNLIGHT

I T WAS A TERRIBLE SATURDAY, the kind of Saturday you have after a Friday night spent explaining to your third wife why you had a hooker in your house and how the condom wrapper she spotted under the couch was not, after all, even necessary. I promised said wife I would get some help. To mark my sincerity, I suggested we all go to a bookstore—wife, son, me. I'd start there. This earned her gruff consent.

I considered changing everything about the way I read, but my remorse ran deeper. I considered changing everything about the way I lived, loved, breathed, and ate as well. I was in that not smoking, not drinking, resume going to Mass place, maybe learn a foreign language and spend a decade reading Dickens place. I would live forever in family. I was in the poorhouse of want and shame, which dogs often call home. It's where I belonged.

In the poetry section, I picked up an anthology edited by Robert Bly—he couldn't have been more disdainful of the kind of work I had loved; I'd always returned the favor. He wanted "story," "emotion," "power," and "love." He wanted language treated as sacred, not something to be torn, shorn, and stripped naked. That's it! That's what I wanted to hear now. Next to Bly was an old favorite—Charles Bernstein, founding Language poet, colleague, friend. On the back of his book, this: "Bernstein's allegiance has not been to any one kind of poetry, but to an 'artificed' writing that refused simple absorption into the society around it." Why would I be interested in that? *Refusing* society? What had that done for me? What was I doing? I took the Bly and dropped Charles back in his slot.

I moved to the self-help section. I stood there in the brightly lit area (it seemed more brightly lit than the poetry section—is that possible?). I found the adoption books, most of them on how to adopt. Or how to search. Being adopted was the source of my problems, I'd grimly announced. My wife approved this line of inquiry. I was on it.

I spotted Betty Jean Lifton's spread of titles on the adoption experience. I opened one of them and found a brief section headed "Literature" toward the back. It dealt solely with the writer Harold Brodkey—"an adoptee who is not involved in the adoption movement." Adoption movement? I decided to leave that part for another time.

Lifton offered up Brodkey as a victim of what she called "the adoption syndrome," and his prose as symptomatic of an adoptee's unwhole self. Brodkey had told her that he "used adoption as a form of freedom—it separates you from the norm."

"Brodkey is all adoptees writ large," she concluded. Adoption, freedom, writing. I leafed inside for more:

"Orphans child heroes—Oedipus, Moses, Sargon, Romulus, Remus and Superman . . . pretended to be real persons in everyday relationships and then disappeared on secret exploits that they shared with no one.

Unless caught.

"Adoptees, then, live with a dual sense of reality, wanted and unwanted, superchild and monsterchild, immortal and mortal. . . . One part is chosen, the other abandoned."

And left on the carpet.

"Adoptee fantasies . . . are an attempt to repair one's broken narrative, to dream it along. They enable the child to stay magically connected with the lost birth mother."

Her name was Cinnamon, she said.

I underlined the words *broken narrative* so hard, I tore through the page: everything I did not know captured in two words—and now it's the only thing I know.

I took the Lifton book, returned the Bly to his slot, picked up the Bernstein again, put it back again, and read in a chair till the rest of the family had made their choices. I had made mine: Lifton, with a promise to find Brodkey.

"AN ACCIDENTAL GLORY." These three words end the first thing I ever read by Harold Brodkey, a story of his called "His Son, in His Arms, in Light, Aloft," long ago. The story appeared in an issue of the *New American Review,* edited by Ted Solotaroff. Long ago was around 1979 or '80, after *NAR* had become defunct, and its slim teal-colored volumes, each bound like a mass-market paperback, could be found in used-book bins all over the city. They made for bargain reading. I was young and new to New York City and its literary culture. I was making $117 a week as a copyeditor for the Institute of Electronic and Electrical Engineers on East Forty-seventh Street.

By the time I arrived at these three words—sitting alone in my fourth-floor walk-up on East Eighty-first Street—I was in tears, breathing hard. That's what I remembered of Harold Brodkey.

"His Son, in His Arms, in Light, Aloft" is about one thing— a son being carried by a father, into and out of sunlight. That's it. In about seven thousand words, you go from "I am being lifted into the air" to the ending, where the sunlight is so bright in the child's eyes that he turns his head inward, toward the heat of his father's neck, and then notices his father's face, "unprotected from the luminousness all around us . . . caught in that light. In an accidental glory."

That passed for love, in Brodkey. It passed for love with me—a tableau, of some relation, in a wider, alien, luminousness, where nothing is fated, nothing is assured; where everything's an accident, but nonetheless glorious.

I was particularly vulnerable to that kind of thing at that time: My little boy, from my first marriage, not yet two years old, and his mother, after trying to live with me, had decamped for Indiana, where she was from and where we had met three years earlier. Together, she and I had endured a romantic collision at the end of my senior year of college, gotten married at an outdoor hippie/Chicano civil ceremony that August, complete with roasted pig, Mexican rock band (Los Impactos), and plenty of psilocybin; we'd braved a year in Leeds, England, as I worked toward a master's degree; survived my parents' disapproval of our marriage and then enjoyed their blessing when my son was born; but we couldn't handle eighteen months of being poor and unaccomplished and kid-burdened, and we came apart. Though one part of me was giddy with the freedom of being single again and not strapped by nightly, suffocating family affairs and grinding domestic chaos, I missed my little boy.

I might have seen Brodkey not long after. I was sitting in my local Irish bar, where I stretched out five dollars nearly every night into eight or nine mugs of draft beer with a dollar's tip, mourning my losses by forgetting them. A man wearing the face I'd seen pictured in a copy of *Esquire,* with the long, solid, beveled head and accusing eyes, came through the door, his cashmere coat swinging from his broad shoulders like the cape of a warrior, a garment he seemed to expect someone would relieve him of, so that then he could fire off a few quick combinations like a fighter, or, presto, produce a handkerchief from a sleeve and release a dove. An elegant woman with a cap of short silvery hair followed in his wake, looking bemused. She did not remove his coat and they did not stay for a drink, as I had hoped. Harold bulled his way to the bar and asked—a bit imperiously of Leo, the barman, I thought—directions to some place he was clearly not in. Snow melted and winked out on the wool of his topcoat. I thought of saying something about his story or something clever in the literary-gossip category—"What's up with Joseph Heller? I read it. *Nothing* happened!"—but I was in my cups, so I swallowed it. Through the bar's large window I could see the two of them on Second Avenue, looking north. Harold donned a hat I had not seen—a fedora; he snapped the brim as if setting a course, put his arm around his lady, and together they sailed forth.

That was the last I thought of Harold Brodkey for the next sixteen or seventeen years, during which time I built a career in publishing, wrote a few books, married again, and then again; cycled out of New York for brief stints—for a small literary press in Dutchess County, for the editorship of a magazine about small literary presses, in Connecticut—and generally filled my reading with writers who were not Harold Brodkey. I could hardly be faulted for abandoning Harold: During this time, if he was known at all, it was for *not* publishing. Something about a long-promised novel, announced more than once in publisher catalogs, had continually failed to appear, its nonexistence moving from house to house, looking for a home that would have it, for a house that would wait for its author to finish, pronounce it done. When it did come, the reviews were dismissive: *The Runaway Soul.* I did not read it.

Could I be faulted for abandoning my young son? He was now a teenager; he lived in Indiana. He had two younger half brothers. I saw them all at his mother's funeral—my first wife's funeral. She died brutally of hypothermia, alone, drunk, in a cold January rain. Could I be faulted for having moved on, to other marriages, now my third, with a new son? These questions hadn't vexed me much, but they would. And they turned me back to Harold Brodkey—with an assist from that small tear of condom-wrapper foil, detritus from a drunken night alone in the city when the family was away.

Over the years, I had maintained a respect for the Brodkey style that I remembered from the father-son story, not to mention a notion of literary celebrity from that sighting in the bar, even if I'd only imagined it. I knew there weren't other stylists working like that, endlessly circling a subject or a feeling, spending an entire story on one small shaft of sunlight and those it falls upon, pushing people, the same people, in and out of it, and writing about it. There was a rawness of emotion in what I sensed in his work; not coarse, like Harry Crews or Charles Bukowski, but deeply nuanced, like very complicated surgery into emotion's entrails—Henry James–like, but speedy, neurotic, modern. I was wary of it. Still, I was too engaged, during those years, in other projects of reading and coping and not coping, to follow what Brodkey was (not) up to. Then that night and the penitential bookstore visit that followed.

I PROCEEDED TO READ ALL OF BRODKEY—the two slim volumes of stories, the huge story collection (*Stories in an Almost Classical Mode*), the novel *The Runaway Soul,* the Venice novel, *Profane Friendship;* the outtakes from *PF* (*My Venice*); the nonfiction essays and reviews, *Sea Battles on Dry Land;* and the final statement about his approaching death, as detailed in *The New Yorker*—and I decided I had no sympathy for him. Inside the front cover of one of his books, I scribbled, "HB: So incapable of forgiveness himself that his principle project is to so irk the reader as to make the reader unforgiving, too. Now we're all guilty."

Brodkey was famously prickly; by most accounts, vain and preening. He was a braggart in his books—about his genius, his prick, his luck "in sex, in looks"—and he comes off as simply asinine. He thought he was original and brave and at the end declared himself "tired of defending my work." Tired he may have been, but there is no defending the author of so many confused, contradictory, obnoxious, ill-kempt and self-important paragraphs that tumor his work. Like this, from *Runaway Soul*:

> *The thing about the absolute and the artists who made art out of it is that the only structure they have which generates emotion is the structure of the awesomeness of the absolute and then the curiously moving pain and comedy of the mind wandering as it inevitably does in real moments, in the immensities of the real; and I prefer the structures of actual emotion and the reality of moments.*

It's a shame that Brodkey's excesses were not reined in, because what he was after—"making conscious language . . . deal with wild variability . . . by telling a story in reference to real time"—is a laudable project, one pursued by only a few major practitioners—Proust, Stein, Kerouac. And it led to some remarkable literary feats—his infamous story "Innocence," about bringing a woman to her first orgasm, a thirty-two-page story, fifteen thousand words, some of them laughable, some of them memorable ("To see her in sunlight was to see Marxism die"), full of Brodkey's obnoxious self-regard, but also, a rare ride along, in prose, with someone thinking and feeling and, in this case, fucking. True, it was sensationalist, but in a way it was the perfect Brodkey story arc—a steady state of want/desire accompanied by physicality and talk ending in a climax.

I MET BRODKEY ONCE, and it was perhaps the boldest thing I have ever done, and one that I may have yet to answer for in some literary afterlife—a wild aesthetic gambit born of desperation. I knew from Lifton, whom I began to see as a therapist, that Brodkey was sick; and then I knew from *The New Yorker* ("I have AIDS. I am surprised that I do.") what he was sick from. I knew from Lifton where he lived, and who his wife was. I had many questions, complaints, and compliments to offer, and I decided to call Ellen Schwamm Brodkey, Harold's wife. She answered the phone. Her voice was heavy, as if imitating a man's. If it was playful, it was play with an edge. "Hel-lo—o-o," she said, and dragged it out, near peevish, a note or two—as if to say, Make this good. Or good-bye.

I said who I was and what I wanted—to talk to her husband about his writing and adoption; that I was adopted—she cut me off with some guttural sound. I assumed it was with purpose. I went silent. She was silent. Then I heard a croaky, "What is it?" It was Harold. His syllables crumbled into air like a day-old baguette. Wispy. Again, I said who I was and what I wanted; I was an admirer of his work and hoped to talk to him about his writing and—he cut me off, but this was for a cough, a long cough that was going to cost him dearly in precious breath. I could hear a gasping receding from the phone.

"Do you mind hanging on," said Ellen, back on. I realized then, as I waited, hearing the howling run of Harold's coughing, that these were fucking tough people. "No, no," I said. "Should I call—" She cut me off again. "He does this. He'll get over it. Honey, now . . ." I could hear her say, love in her voice as his awful hoarse huffing began to subside.

They invited me to come up and visit on the following Sunday. "The newspapers bring him to life, and then he is talkative—aren't you, Harold—especially the *Book Review*," she said, laughing, at his expense, I felt. I heard a squawk from him and wondered what I was in for.

It was going to be a big event for me, and my wife knew it. She had welcomed my efforts at reform as a promising start. She suggested I take some time to myself on Saturday—"do what you have to do"—to prepare for Sunday's assignation. I took a couple of his books—the early stories and the one just out then, *Profane Friendship*, a novel (his second; all of a sudden—written, I heard, in nine months!)—and some clippings I'd found, and a notebook for notes, and I set off for the New York Public Library. I got as far as the Lion's Head, about forty blocks short.

I remember sitting in the sunlight that spilled in off Christopher Street. It was late fall, a near winter light, the low southern sun coming through a leafless Sheridan Square. I loved the way the day's first drink hit, and how the thin, kind light brought out the burl in the bar's rounded rail.

I set to work in the bar. No one was there to bother me, the regulars not up yet, not in. I wrote down question after question for Brodkey. I decided to assure him at the outset that this was to be an inquiry into writing style and its connection (if any) to the experience of adoption. I would take *Profane Friendship* for him to sign. I was certain he loved this book—because it was a clear embrace of love between men, and here he was, dying of AIDS and being accused of being a publicity bitch even as death made its way toward him, and of floating a fallacious chronology of when he got AIDS (in the 1970s, he wrote). I thought immediately, This is a time frame that squares with something he told his wife; he's lying, and I resolved not to ask him about it. "It's your story to tell," I imagined saying to him.

Was this just a fantasy, meeting Harold Brodkey, in his home, to ask these questions? As I lapped at my fourth or fifth Beck's, I got scared. I might blow it off. I might never go. Usually, an idea like this stayed an idea, an imagined conversation, one in which I could ask bold questions, be told clever answers, and never actually have to sit in the humid, live space with another person, in this case an enigmatic stranger who was dying.

I would go there, I decided. I must. I closed my notebook. I moved to the other end of the bar just as a couple of my mates came in, surprised to find me there, and more surprised that I was already well on my way. A long day into evening it was—college football, Clinton jokes. Frank McCourt walked in; over the din, I tried to impress him with my project for the next day with Brodkey. I tried to tell Frank of the broken narrative of the famine survivors. "You're a little cracked there yourself, Michael," he said. He wouldn't say a word about Brodkey. "I hear it's your birthday, is it," he said, and bought me a drink. And it was.

Their apartment on the Upper West Side was like other Upper West Side apartments I'd been in—sudden, intricate warrens of rooms with unaccountable amounts of sunlight within. This was where and how, I had come to feel, a certain professional class from a certain era lived in Manhattan—Jewish, doctors, theater people; the heart of the city's opera and serious drama market; liberal democrats; good people, people who read fiction. People who would take me in.

The doorman announced me and I was sent up. The elevator opened onto a hallway with a mirror over a small table with a bowl of flowers. I looked terrible. I looked dark-eyed and haunted. I looked vulnerable. This is how I wanted to appear to Harold Brodkey.

Ellen answered the door. She was taller than I, her face handsome. She said "Hello, Michael," warmly. She had short white hair, enormous bangle earrings. She was made up. There were hoops upon hoops of a silk blouse around her neck and upper body; Capri pants and slippers. She was lovely.

I made my way in. No Harold.

I was offered coffee or tea. "Coffee, black," I said. Harold was to be brought out by a nurse, Ellen informed me. I heard the radio go silent—she'd clicked it off. That awful Isaiah Sheffer introducing the awful William Hurt.

I held my tongue about Sheffer, whose pompous intoning over a tuning orchestra introduced every week an otherwise-valuable series of short stories on radio. But my mind was slow with yesterday's drink, heavy as a loaf of vinegar-soaked bread. I feared I smelled as bad. I would need to refer to my notes, which were right at hand. Harold rolled into the room.

He was not grizzled; he was shaven. His head looked enormous and dented, as if his skull had suffered an accident and been acceptably banged out in a body shop with rubber mallets. His hair was so short and gray that it was barely distinguishable from his pale skin. The eyes were another matter, though—bright, somehow sharp-edged, as if made of broken glass, and they glittered under eyebrows that were restless.

He smiled crookedly and extended his hand from beneath a beautiful tartan blanket.

"Thank God you came. Life's too short to hear Bill Hurt do Hemingway over into a what? A car salesman."

"I can't stand that show," I blurted out as Ellen handed me coffee in a large French bowl. I needed my two hands to hold it, so I put my books down.

"Let's sit down," Harold said. He cocked his head, amused that, of course, seated he already was.

"So, you're with *Publishers Weekly,* I understand." I hadn't mentioned that. I was an editor there.

"Yes," I admitted.

"You like my book?" he asked, looking at the copy of *Profane Friendship* I had placed on the coffee table.

"I think it is very beautiful. It reminds me of Thomas Mann. It's your *Death in Venice?*" My lip was trembling. I hadn't read Mann's short book, but I had seen the Visconti movie with Dirk Bogarde long ago.

He looked at me and puffed a breath. "I guess you didn't write this, then?" He closed his eyes. "And I quote: 'Brodkey's logorrhea is painful to read, endlessly, strenuously yet tentatively straining for effect; never has a severe editor been more needed. There is a considerable talent here, certainly, but buried in self-indulgence.' "

From memory he did this. I was silent.

"*Publishers Weekly,*" he said.

"Well . . ." I began.

"My editor was hurt." His face broke into all kinds of parts of a smile. Tough all right.

I told him I loved self-indulgence. "Who else can we indulge?" I offered, and he looked approvingly at Ellen, who was busy adjusting the blinds.

"*Whom*," he said with a glance, correcting me.

"We can only try," Ellen said with feigned weariness as the blinds ruffled down loudly.

"Stop," he said.

I rushed to reassure him, this sick man, but came up empty.

"Turgid and self-indulgent, that word again," he said, quoting. "*Publishers Weekly, The Runaway Soul*. You've been hard on me, but I deserve it."

I told him that anyone wrestling to make a sentence convey the movement of thought and feeling in the act of thinking and feeling, not in reflection, but in action, is going to find it hard going. Only real writers appreciate the bravery of the struggle. He liked that.

I began to feel doubts about my own problems with Harold's excesses. If I wanted a writer to follow the movements of thought as they are thought, why should I complain that some of it lacks structure, argument, discipline?

I had to go on. I decided to brave it. "I don't think you do story very well," I said to him, and hastened to add, "I don't, either," as if he gave a shit. "I can't even tell a joke"—my favorite line about this malady.

"Hummph." He made the noise, and I waited. "How to tell a joke . . ." His voice trailed off and his eyes settled on a buttercup of sunlight shimmering on the opposite wall. We both watched it. Ten seconds passed.

"I can't master—and I wonder what you feel about this," I said, pulling out my notebook—"the going from a to b to c; the plot building, the holding back of information in order to build mystery and then delivering it with artful timing."

"That's quite true," he said, and closed his eyes.

Ellen was gone now. The nurse I had seen but for a second was gone as well. The room was silent, the furniture respectfully at ease. He might be falling asleep.

"What do you like—*specifically*—about my work? Tell me." His eyes opened.

"I think 'The River' section of *Runaway Soul* is a brilliant set piece. No one else could have written it."

"It's about jerking off," he said challengingly, "in a river. Who else *would* have written it?"

I said, "Mr. Brodkey, it is about more than . . . jerking off." My hesitation—was it prudery?—brought a look of interest to his face. I think he may have wanted to talk about jerking off, but was intrigued by having the conversation turn, if now it was, to talking about not talking about jerking off.

"It's about sunlight," I ventured, "and shadow and the pull of a river and birdsong and clouds and being a young child, an adopted boy, entering puberty, entering this river—was it the Missouri?—and being afraid that someone, his adoptive father, right?—was about to die, or had died, I can't—"

He cut me off. "Yes, yes, yes. I love that piece. I found such release in it. Do you know," he asked, rolling his chair back a little, "Kafka's story 'The Judgment'?"

Indeed I did! "I do, yes." This was a lucky break. "I know the last line, in fact."

"Really. Well, what is it? I forget."

"'At that moment the traffic was literally frantic.'"

"Yes," he said, closing his eyes again. "Something like that."

There was a long pause before he resumed. I realized he has waiting out the crunching sounds of some trash compacting from the street. "Kafka said that he wrote that story in one sitting, through the night. A father humiliates a son, and the son runs to the train trestle, hangs beneath the bridge, and lets himself go, down into the gorge. The end. He said it was like an orgasm when he wrote that last sentence—*literally frantic.*"

This had to be the end of the interview. I wanted to run out of there. It was too perfect. But I couldn't. There was nowhere to run to; there were tears in my eyes. I felt vivid.

Without composure, I said, "Is that the perfect story, then? One that follows an emotion into some kind of . . . release? Death? Or"—I hazarded it—"ejaculation?"

Harold suddenly seemed tired. His eyes were at half-mast. "Yes, I suppose so. It's the best we can do. But not enough."

Ellen brought some scones out, and offered lemonade. "Fruit only for you, Harold." She placed a bowl of melon cubes in his lap.

I crumbled through a scone while Harold sucked at the melon bits. We recovered, for it seemed we had to.

"What else did you want to ask?" he said, and I felt the shadow of the nurse behind me.

"I wanted to know, sir," I replied, adopting for no good reason a jocular tone, "if you felt that not having a complete uninterrupted story to your life, because of the adoption and being raised by, what, a second cousin to your father and her husband in a weird place like University City, Missouri, you were unable to write—or was it *uninterested* in writing—a conventional narrative, something beyond the template of, say, sexual *coming*. Some of your stories follow the same path."

He was silent for a time. I stopped chewing my scone.

"Uninterested," he said. "Ergo unable."

As I descended in the elevator, I realized I had forgotten to have him sign my book. In fact, I had left it there. When the doorman showed me the street, the sunlight was blinding. I stared into the sun's wide glare for the second I could stand it, then dropped my lids. An explosion of reds, sheets of Rubylith and sea life, in a flood.

I Thought You Were Dale

It was Delia in produce who told Carla about the guy who'd moved in down by the lake. Took over the condo when old Mrs. Beauharnois died, might've been a cousin or a nephew or something, Delia said. He's a widow, she said.

Er, said Carla. It's widow*er*.

That's when Carla got to thinking—out of the blue—that she just might, someday, in her own way—in her own time— might make a move on this guy Dale Sweeney, though she'd never laid eyes on him.

Carla was on the rebound from Jeff. She still felt young, only thirty, not too worn if you didn't look too close. Worked off the baby fat. She'd check herself out mornings in the ceiling mirror Jeff had installed—a little harder around the edges, she thought, from work and worry, of course. She liked the look—kind of a fuzzy Madonna look after she'd found Pilates. And Carla'd started reading her books a little again. Ayn Rand. Terry McMillan. Danielle Steel.

So what if Jeff had split. Good riddance to bad rubbish. He left the truck; at least there's that, Carla reasoned. Let him drive the little goddamn broken-down old Datsun to his shit job at Wendy's and his girlfriend's dump on Rugar Street. That's rich: Had to go find himself, and he finds himself all right—over in Wiggletown. And sinking.

On the other hand . . . *Carla on the upswing!* Nice pro-
motion at Price Chopper, new responsibilities, the pinstripe
shirt and blue skirt rather than the sweatshirt and hairnet
deal in bakery. Plus a raise—up to $10.50 now. And she just
loved that clipboard she had to carry around; she even kept
it with her in the truck, the thing sliding around on the
dashboard importantly. And her kids weren't fucked-up like
most kids in this situation; not yet. They had Grandma and
school and they loved their room now that Jeff had finally
put down the purple carpet.

DELIA, TALL AND BROAD as a cigar store Indian, saw everyone
come in the store from her spot in produce. Everybody had to
walk through there—aisles of fruit on the left, veggies on the
right—before they got to anything else they might really want.
There were really good scientific reasons for this, Mr. Crevecoeur said so, and said someday she, Carla, could read up on
it in the company literature that he kept in a binder in his
office. There was a word for this, but Carla couldn't remember
what it was, but whatever it was, basically it explained why
you buried the things people were most likely to be coming
in wanting—milk, beer, meat—at the back of the store, so
they'd have to walk through the things they might not really
want or'd rather forget they were supposed to get—like peas
and carrots. Whatever. Carla was somewhat interested.

Delia had come up to the desk early last Saturday and
said to Carla, Looky-who, and nodded over her shoulder.
Which one? said Carla. With the cute butt, said Delia, and
that little giddyup there, that limp. Delia pronounced with
a flourish, *I give you . . . Dale Sweeney.*

Carla saw him. He did have a cute ass, in worn jeans. His

limp—yes, he did have one—was more of a swivel, to the discerning eye. He had a big wallet in his rear-end right pocket, and a chain swung from that down and then up toward his front somewhere. She could see an old faded bandana spilling a little from his rear-end left pocket. He wore a jean jacket.

They watched Dale Sweeney lean over to pick up a rutabaga from the basket. He brought it to his nose and sniffed. He then held the rutabaga nearly at arm's length in his right hand, admiring the root vegetable. He had large hands. With his thumb, he worked away the wax on the purple rim, and then took another sniff. Why, he's a gourmet, Carla thought. Then he bent down quickly—Carla saw only the smallest of love handles on his hips, white as pork—and put the rutabaga back. Pick-EEE! She and Delia exchanged looks.

Dale Sweeney continued on down the aisle, past all the lettuces—the iceberg, the Boston, the romaine, the Bibb, the frizzy shit, the mixed mesclun bin—before Mr. Crevecoeur said, Carla, c'mere, dear. Also: Delia, problem? No, sir. Just needed a price check on the rutabagas. She shuffled off. Carla could see little leaves of whaddyacall-it—watercress—pressed into the white underside of Delia's fat forearms like little shamrocks.

Carla, said Mr. Crevecoeur. Yuh, said Carla, resigned to not seeing her man till perhaps he swung out of produce, moved along smoked meats, and then headed right up aisle two—coffee, teas, specialty—and there she'd see the face of the man she already loved, with the nice ass and the adorable hobble.

Carla?

Uh, yessir.

Do you watch TV? Mr. Crevecoeur seemed to be squinting at her, or perhaps it was a slow-moving wink in process.

Carla surprised herself with a quick and very effective reply: Of course not. I can't. I mean, migraines, sir.

Right, of course, of course, he said, his mind stalling. How old are you?

Carla gave him a look that said, You're out of line. Old enough, she said.

Of course, said Mr. Crevecoeur. Who's that out there you and Delia Heffer are so fascinated with? He removed his glasses to work at a smear on the lens with his thumb and forefinger, but he just made it worse. His left eye was dripping.

Weirdo, she thought, turning to go back to the customer service desk, her clipboard across her belly. It made her feel . . . professional, like a doctor with his charts. Her charts.

Do you know his name? asked Mr. Crevecoeur from behind her.

Carla turned around. No, she said. What are you talking about? Who?

Mr. Crevecoeur put his glasses back on and gave his head a little shake, as if he were clearing water from goggles after a swim.

Pay no attention to me, Darla, he said. And then he started his strange laugh, more like a sniveling sound.

It's *Carla,* Mr. Crevecoeur.

That's what I said, he replied, with a cracked grin that looked painful. As he walked away, she thought she heard him mutter that he thought *she* was Dale! She thought he said, *I thought you were Dale!* Dale Sweeney? How could that be? She let it drop.

She took a cigarette break on that one, standing out back, where the old cracked-up tarmac looked like a map of strange countries, like Africa.

CARLA FIGURED SHE WAS SMARTER than your average Price Chopper employee. She was a Regents Scholar and took calculus once. She was a woman who knew her way around, who knew how to get what she wanted from a man, so she didn't need to talk to the likes of Big Delia or anybody else at work or at the gym, where she sculpted her butt. She could handle it. She had a plan.

Her plan was this: Dale Sweeney's new place was just up the lake from the Yacht Club, which had a decent brunch on the weekends. JayPee and Callie were old enough now to eat cereal on their own and watch their shows in the morning, so that would give Carla a good start on what she called intelligence gathering. She'd cruise down to the Yacht Club for a modest breakfast—brunch—on the deck in back (no fries). She would eat alone. People would understand, what with Jeff just having left. Just about everybody knew it, didn't they? From there, from that big round table in the corner of the back room, looking north up the lake shore, she is sure she could see Dale Sweeney's condo. She could probably see the sliding doors to his living room. Could probably see his TV and through the archway into his kitchen!

BILLY AT THE BAR GAVE CARLA A HARD TIME. She showed up at ten-thirty and there was no one in the place. Where's the brunch crowd? she asked him.

Been out all night, Car? I heard about Jeff.

She knew it: Everybody *did* know!

Carla made it clear to Billy that her comings and goings weren't any of his biz, but now she was busy killing time, like, did she really want to sit here and have brunch in an empty dining room with Billy at the stick and she wasn't even hungry? No. And how would she get away with sitting there looking at Dale's condo without it being pretty clear she was sitting there looking up the lake at Dale's condo? So she asked when the Bills game was on and was told that the pregame began in about forty-five minutes. She asked if the newspaper was around and if the kitchen was open yet and whether or not they were still suffering from the exchange rate. Main thing to avoid was Billy giving her the first degree. He was a sweet-enough guy, but he used to be a psych major, so everything was mom and dad, and whatever you said you didn't want was really you saying what you did want, according to Dr. Billy.

What'll you have?

Carla hesitated. She didn't want anything but a pair of binoculars and, maybe, a Percoset.

How about a Bloody Mary? A bullshot?

There was no use telling Billy no—to him, it meant yes.

She ordered a Bloody Mary, even though it wasn't noon yet and it wasn't legal, and took a menu and went back to the sunny area in the back room. And there it was. One, two, three condos up the lake. His jeans were actually hanging on a clothesline.

She still hadn't really seen Dale up close—his face, that is. Not of recent vintage anyway. She and Delia had looked through a bunch of old yearbooks from his school, where, as it happens, Delia's cousin was once the nurse and so had all the books from a certain era. And there he was, Dale X. Sweeney, class of '84. Blondish hair upswept at the temples, a scattering of freckles, high, sharp cheekbones to die for, eyes a little beady, to be honest, like maybe he was a car thief. He really looked more 1950s than 1980s, more duck's ass than disco. Can't see no teeth, said Big Delia, which was true. I assume he's got 'em, said Carla.

Carla had barely touched her Bloody Mary when Billy came over. It's a bye week, actually, he said. There ain't no Bills game today.

Wow, thought Carla. How interesting.

She teased him. Billy, you're so . . . honest with me. It's like we was brother 'n' sister. *Were*, she corrected herself, silently.

No, he said. I mean, I meant, you know, there's not likely, um, to, you know, like the crowd, it'll be a slow one today. Not much for me is what I'm saying.

Really, said Carla in a deadpan.

It's nice to see you is all, said Billy, moving away from her table back to the bar.

She drew the straw of her drink to her lips and sucked a good jolt of vodka from the bottom. She let the warmth of the sun off the lake through the porch glass glint off her cheeks and toast her lightly. She gazed at Dale Sweeney's jeans doing a slow cowboy's dance in the wind.

Nothing came of that but a headache from the second cocktail she had, plus the Marlboro she smoked in the parking lot before heading home to make lunch for JayPee and Callie. Carla went back the following Saturday, and there was a bit of a crowd for a college game of some sort—she couldn't care less; college football was all southern wasn't it, like NAS-CAR?—but no sign of Dale, not even his pants. She went again the next Sunday, pretending a little interest in someone she knew would never be there—an old flame from a distant town, who, she knew, had moved to Colorado. But she told Billy he might be in—this guy—on Sunday, explaining her presence once again. But no Dale.

She decided, This sweetie pie doesn't come home or doesn't get up till afternoon, now does he? I'm too early in this brunch deal. So she made a quick change of plans. The Bills are the Monday-night game, yeah, Billy?

Why *yass*, he said with a leer.

Out the door she went.

Right then, of course—like clockwork!—Carla's mom's colostomy bag broke—really, right about then, because when she got home, JayPee said Grandma had called and to call her right away.

She couldn't believe it. The bag had blown in the living room, where Carla's mom had leaned over to adjust the TV set, and the bladder got squashed between her thigh and her midriff and—you know—all over the TV screen and that perforated speaker plate and, of course, the pile carpet she and Jeff had given her for Christmas a year ago. There was even shit high up on the brass clockworks on top of the TV, right on the underside of the hat brim of the bronze cowboy on the bronze horse. Shit bronze: amazing to behold, amazing that Carla noticed. But she was superwoman, anything for her mom today. Carla got there in ten minutes and brought her own bucket and mop and ammonia.

Things got worse, of course, the next day. Carla stopped off at Dragoon's to get a resupply of bags and a fresh *TV Guide*. They watched *Meet the Press* together, but her mom got sicker as Sunday afternoon began to fade. Carla finally left at eight to get back to the kids and give them dinner and baths, but she knew she would be back. Sure enough, her mother called at eleven, saying she needed EMS. She had a fever, her stoma was infected, and she had cramps. Nice progress.

As Carla drove to her mother's, she was proud that she knew what a stoma was, thanks to Mr. Crevecoeur. Somehow it had come up months ago, in the employee lounge—someone else's mother maybe—and Mr. C. said it meant mouth in Greek. Stomach, he said, was really a big mouth. The doctor just gives you another mouth. Everyone thought, What? Colostomy means colon mouth, said Mr. C. carefully.

IT WAS TRICKY GETTING BIG DELIA to sit with the kids on Monday night, but Carla finessed it. She ran a guilt trip on Big D. You're the one who got me all interested in this guy, she said. Just let me do my thing.

What's your thing, Car?

You never mind.

Carla's mom was all set up in a semiprivate room. John's coverage from the prison was still top-notch, even though he'd died six years ago. As a surviving spouse, Marie qualified. She assured Carla she was just fine; she liked the woman in the bed next to her—an Indian from the reservation with failing kidneys; they both liked the soaps.

Carla had to put in half a day at Ye Old Price Chop, as Mr. Crevecoeur called it at the company party after a couple of Buds, before beginning her prep for Monday night. She expected an easy half shift; Mr. C.'d be doing his inventory. But instead, there he was in customer service with a bandage on his head. He was jabbering when Carla signed in; again she thought he was maybe talking to her and maybe not. Sir? she said.

Darla, er, Carla, he began. *I thought you were Dale!* He said it with a theatrical flourish and a southern twang.

Carla was confused. I'm just signing in; half day today, sir. Bakery.

You just don't know. You're so young. A TV commercial.

We were all saying it: *I thought, I thought you were Dale!* He laughed and then winced. His head hurt, you could tell.

I said bakery, said Carla, clarifying.

It was a Grape-Nuts commercial, actually. A teenage boy. Underwater. Now listen: A teenage boy underwater, he pushes a woman in a bathing suit to the surface. Splashing everywhere. She lets out a yelp! Turns out it wasn't that young buck's girlfriend—Dale—but her mother. And he says, *But, but, I thought, I thought you were Dale!*

Mr. Crevecoeur laughed. Carla started tapping her foot like she did when she got impatient. You know why? You know why he thought she was Dale? I'll tell you.

Because she ate Grape-Nuts and had a nice figure, offered Carla as a guess.

Mr. C. closed both eyes, as if waiting to pass something painful. Carla headed off to the bakery.

SHE GOT A LIGHT FROST FROM DEBBIE'S HAIR WE ARE and then took a step class at the Comfort Inn for a little tone and to give a slight humid jostle to her locks. She took a long shower at home (with shower cap) and imagined Dale looking at her through the frosted glass. I don't need to eat Grape-Nuts, she thought, if that's what it was. Then she sat on the edge of the toilet seat, wrapped in a towel, her skin pink and tingling in the way that happy skin slowly cooling tingles, and she waited. Carla felt she could wait forever in just this phase—this transitional stage. She wasn't wet and she wasn't dry; the mirror was fogged, though she could see the shadow of the shape of her head through the clouded surface; she was not single and she was not married; her parents were alive, and dead; she was and was not a lot of things, and in there, in between things, she felt free. She wondered why she wanted to change a thing about her life. These were interesting thoughts to her. Suddenly, she was afraid her cell phone would ring—she turned it off. She locked the door—she could hear the scramble of cartoon noises with kids' laughter mixed in; they'd be content for hours; they could pee upstairs when they needed to. Carla turned the tub faucet back on, hot. She wanted more steam to rise. For a few moments, she hung over the tub itself, letting her towel loosen, and tickling with her fingers her own neck beneath her ringlets. Chills rose from within her, only to be satisfyingly warmed and melted at her skin's surface. She could hardly get enough of this.

Carla sat back on the flipped-down toilet seat and decided that Mr. Crevecoeur was scary—maybe gay without knowing it, which was the scary part, and no way was she going to a bar for *Monday Night Football*, Dale or no Dale. No way was she going. No way she was going anywhere, and she let the water run.

Then she remembered: Delia was coming over to baby-sit. Carla turned off the water and began pawing through a drawer, looking for her eyelash curler. By the time she found it, the mirror had cleared. She sat there, batting her eyes, flirting with herself, trying to imagine the moment of her arrival and how her life would look if she were Dale.

INN OF THE NATIONS

EVERY MORNING WAS A REVELATION, a new idea, for Father Paul Connolly, S.J., pastor at Church of the Assumption in Oreville. And this morning was no different. It was true—and a possible sermon topic?—waking up each day, today such a day, with an insight into how it all worked, God's great machine, those big gears and spheres of time and space and decency, all bathed in grace like an oil, though . . . Was that the idea? Never mind, thought Father Paul. The creep of the secular, the monsignor is right. Next.

Nonetheless, the revelation. . . . No, he *had* already forgotten it. That was fast. Few things live as short a life as that did! Marvelous. There's something, though, left: Perhaps every morning the revelation needs to be refreshed. Yes, part of something to live for, the search renewing every day. Father Paul, now warming: For to wake up two days or three days in a row or a lifetime of days, as the monsignor himself has often boasted (as if it were true, as if it were good), *with the same idea* is to be . . . coerced. Deluded. One loses the necessary doubt. That'll do it. Thomas. Can work that in at Easter.

Where is the moon? Father Paul wants to know. Writers make note of the moon, don't they? They know not why. He rolls over, or tries to; twisted sheets *cross him like a sash*, he thinks. Not bad. Or a straitjacket. In room 11 of the Inn of the

Nations motel, he struggles to undo the leather belt around his ankle. Small welt. Father Paul wants to get to his book, BOMC's latest insistence.

But the birds are singing, beginning to repeat themselves. Now there's a group waking up to the same revelation every morning and telling it! And worth a listen. Yes, listen: same short stanzas of tweets and warbles . . . sealed with a screech . . . over and over. Undetectable variations—perhaps a musician (he thinks of one: *oh so fondly*) would know them, not Paul. In any event, the same slight changes, day after day, from break of day till midmorning, when, apparently, the appropriate number of iterations have been met. Like saying the rosary. Or reading office. Done when done. If done.

Where's it gotten the birds? Show me the boid who signs his own soong, in his own voice.

Not even our Lord had his own voice. Where is the Book of Jesus? Where's the book of the enlightened Nazarene? Imagine that . . . if it were so. We get close in John—but John, you'd think, was counsel to one very slippery client, not to an honest carpenter.

And now the president is dead.

Father Paul undoes the balky buckle and tosses the cinch to the floor. It rattles across the pine planks and shatters the cheap silence ($12.50 a night). Pine floor, pine wainscoting, gingham curtains, a plain bed, birch-bark lampshades on the night tables, Margaret's green 7 Up bottle atop the TV. He will not turn it on.

When Father Paul's two bare feet hit the floor, he has the sensation he's stepped onto the spinning world. Madness to think this way all the time. No wonder we gave it to Galileo Galilei. Stoning? He can't remember.

Father Paul—his feet and ankles and heart now cold—gets back in bed.

He thinks of Margaret and her harp, *fondly*. Canted between her legs, her slender fingers rippling the air. With . . . heavenly music. Where has Margaret gone?

She'd said, "No." She'd said no over and over, no, no, no, no, no, no, no, no till it is what no is, a refusal, and she said it until it is what no becomes, surrender. The Church is one big no, isn't it? And then the surrender: The flock obeys.

He'd had to nearly force her into the car. Fortunately, they were in the carport, where the other sisters could not see— their only blind spot!—and Mike Seeney was far down the hill turning the grave for Silas Liberty. The world was glued to their TV sets.

"Margaret, now," he said, meant to soothe, meant to direct. "We'll be late."

For what? she should have asked. What would Father Paul say to that? Put that into words, Brother Hopkins. "Wreck of the Deutschland." Okay: *Sister, a sister calling / A master, her master and mine!— / And the inboard seas run swirling and hawling . . .*

Five nuns drown. For a great poem.

They got in the old Packard, the best this parish could do, though how Father Paul had coveted that Fairlane Bob Guerin dangled on Palm Sunday. One day maybe—if monsignor could see to the minuscule down payment and not insist on another auctioneer in his rolling hurdy-gurdy voice— on church grounds!—selling old doors and rotted window frames for the "pastoral car fund." *Gawd.*

The Packard was deep like a carriage, or like that rickety gondola at the county fair. And no radio—a relief today. All the talk of Dallas and the president dead and Johnson shot too? Could that be true?

"Margaret, please calm down." She was shaking. Her small nose pinkened, her cheeks rashed.

She simply could not speak and did not want to speak, and, after a while, cruising along the river, Father Paul thought this is what life among the Carmelites must be like, and then he changed his mind—silence was fine—by the time they reached the new freeway south. It had been a nice day, but now the sky was glowering and early dark was beginning to sift in. A cover.

They made a funny couple . . . if someone knew, but no one did. Father Paul longed for it all to be known, though: his need for immersion in another person, his mingling there, and how good it was for his soul and for his fellowship, meeting the secular halfway; how good it was for his health and strength, so necessary to serving his flock; the Jack LaLanne "Trimnastics" his weekday secret, exercising with his prie-dieu, his little hobbyhorse; did he want it to be known, his trouble with sanctity? All in God's eyes. Did God know? Father Paul often wondered why he still lived.

They weren't a funny couple.

"Justice was done." He said this to her, meant to console. Not a single car on the road.

This elicited a measure of conversation—a derisive sound, not a snort, but something issued from deep within Margaret that she then squelched, angrily, resignedly, a punch pulled. She's better than that. He went on. "I'm not sure I agree with Kennedy's politics," he said, trying on casual.

"He's dead," said Margaret.

"Of course."

"*Agreed,* then. Not *agree.* You the writer."

"That was mean," she added. He could not see her in the backseat, but he could hear her crying.

WHERE DID IT ALL BEGIN? In the beginning.

Paul Connolly, the elder of two children born to John and Joyce (Dugan) Connolly, a star athlete and student in an old mill town, received the call one day in the spring of his junior year. By then, his father had long been dead—a steam joint blew on a dryer at the mill when Paul was eight—a brutal scalding. The mortician replaced Paul Connolly Sr.'s eyes with glass. Paul Junior became his mother's partner, the ardent scholar athlete and Boy Scout. His future, to that point, had been set—or assumed: he would attend Normal School in the county seat; he would be a teacher—perhaps English and gym—and he'd hunt and fish and read *Life* and *Time* and probably marry Jill Chilton, with whom he'd attended two proms. Paul himself assumed that intimacy with a female would begin and end with Jill Chilton, though it had not begun. They would consummate their union, perhaps in a small hotel in Montreal or in Niagara Falls, and have children. But on a cold April Saturday morning—it would have been his father's birthday—Paul worked his tackle in the Black River, just like his father had shown him, when a shadow fell across him, and then fell across the sun. He thought it was a bird of prey, an osprey intent on him. He staggered on the riverbank, cold, frightened. Maybe I am epileptic, he thought, like Ronnie Gonyea, whom he'd seen ride out a fit sitting in his truck, his head flailing up and down in silence—then everything began to rush at him, and then he was in the river. It was high and fast. Paul rose to the surface, but his waders became snagged in branches at the bottom. He was held there in the current, the water to his chin and then higher. Only the flat of his face was out of the water, a floating mask staring at the swirling gray above, the small gnats a fresh hatch to outlive him, and he prayed for his soul. For minutes. If he tried to move, he pulled himself under. Then he tried to pull himself under, to free himself from the swollen waders or break off tree branches, but his hands were numb. He surrendered to this entrapment. He stared downstream, only his nose and brow above water, not daring to open his mouth to shout. He thought, I will drown. He thought, I will die in a river. That is appropriate. And then the sun opened a hole in the cloud, making him blink, and the river shifted beneath him. He spilled into a pool downstream, his gullied waders pulling him onto a shallow sandbar, where he gathered himself, and walked out, saying, "Your will, not mine."

That was 1950. It came out of the blue, literally—the clearing sky—but in other respects it was no surprise, at least to Paul. He'd suffered a period of near-fanatical (but private) devotion to prayer, secretly saying grace before and after every meal (sometimes every course; for a while—one Lent—after every swallow); his evening prayers, too, were forced to be completely imagined in every word—no thoughtless, rote recitation for Paul: Each word of each prayer had to be visualized as both word and a corresponding image ("fruit of thy womb, Jesus" was a high-wire construction involving an apple where something else should be).

His still-grieving mother welcomed his vocation, as if she deserved it. They were good Irish Catholics, after all; it was a fine tradition to give one son to the Church, even if your only son. Fortunately, his sister, Sarah, could bear the grandchildren. Father Paul would baptize them.

Girlfriend Jill ("A.F.A." she had written in his yearbook

under her own picture) eased her way out of Paul's future—a combination of Paul treating her, on a hammock, to a deadly disquisition on Teilhard de Chardin, and then the late-closing suitor with a milk route and a sporty, black, two-door Studebaker, Gordy Gregory, who won her heart. So the four-star athlete and smart boy left for the Korean War, a stint, however, cut short (a misunderstanding in the PX; discharge); then a B.A. in philosophy from the University of the State of New York and a certificate in philosophy from Wadhams Hall College, a seminary up on the St. Lawrence River. On his ordination day in 1958, he took his mother and sister to see a dam come down—what was called "inundation day" for the valley, which would see ten villages sacrificed in the name of progress. He had changed out of the cream and gold of the ceremony into the simple black cassock and black biretta he favored like a boy might. He was severe; his mother, in a feathered hat, dotty; his sister, hatless, and in a bright green suit rather too jaunty for the setting. They saw the explosion at the dam, and then heard it; and then saw the slow hemorrhage of dark water flood the countryside.

"A big day," Paul said to his stricken mother.

"What are you talking about?"

"The river is too shallow," said Paul.

"Too shallow for what?" asked his mother. "For drowning?"

Paul swallowed hard. "For tankers. They're going to build locks."

"For what?"

"One needs to get from here to there, all over. Cargo, freighters."

Masonry crumbling. His mother turned away.

MARGARET TOOK A DIFFERENT PATH in the same direction. She came from farther north, from Quebec City. She was an only child who lost her mother to a street accident when she was only six. Her father was a civil engineer, building bridges, and brought a young woman in to help with Margaret. Margaret loved Mireille, who taught her to dance and bake bread and comb and braid her thick auburn hair. Mireille was also a bit of a rebel—Margaret's father called her a *flambeuse*, a risk taker, because she smoked and had *beaucoup petit copain*—boys.

Margaret's father was strict enough, but not too much. He was gentle toward his little Marguerite, but he hated the Protestant English and the Catholic Mohawks. One day in Vieux Ville—as if the whole city weren't old—her father ran into a Mohawk he knew from work on the Taschereau suspension, who was out with his family. He spoke harshly to the man. The Mohawk had a rosary around his neck, and was drunk. Margaret's father berated the big man, who was ashamed and sought no trouble, but Margaret's father would not stop. She began to scream for him to stop. She pulled on his sleeve. He slapped her, and then punched the Mohawk in the ear. The man fell. Her father then kicked him down the rough cobblestone. Margaret thought, Father, you will go to hell. She said to him, *Allez en enfer!* Her father looked at her, stricken. He could not catch his breath. They made their way toward the cathedral, but once they reached the steep steps, Margaret's father sat down slowly. He put his cheek on the limestone, frothed pink bubbles, and convulsed, looking at his only daughter. Margaret was twelve years old. She went silent then for many months. She thought she would go to hell, but she did not go to hell and made sure she wouldn't. She went to the Ursulines, the teaching order of Catholic nuns that ran a boarding school in a convent at the top of the cliff.

Margaret learned ornamental tapestry making, weaving threads of gold and silver—tapestry being the Ursuline's principal service to the iconography of the Church. Margaret's specialty was in structuring reliefs out of horsehair—the outcropping upon which a saint might stand, the roll of a bishop's miter, the breast and shoulder—and this Margaret felt most fitting—of a horse. But she also learned chemistry and hygiene and German; she learned how to read music and to play the harp—Purcell's *Ode to St. Cecilia,* she practiced for a year. At nineteen she was married to Christ in a wedding dress with a dozen other girls, all of them homely in homely glasses but for Margaret, who was slender and small-boned, her green eyes bright with belief and her French braid curled on her shoulder like a reminder of who she once had been.

When Margaret arrived at Franklin Manor—a former sanatorium and now an Ursuline convent in northern New York—Father Paul, the pastor, saw her by accident one morning her first week there—he'd not had a formal introduction to the new sister. She was down in the laundry; she had taken off her habit and wimple and scapular. Her hair was short, rough-cut, and the color of brass. She had on only a loose white shift. She was bone white. Father Paul could see her breasts moving against the fabric as she worked her arms around, putting clothes into the washer. Her whole upper body tensed and flexed as she ran bedclothes through the ringer, turning the crank round and round. She thought she was alone and unseen in her exertions, didn't she? A private ecstasy. Or did she know that the priest next door across the lawn could see right through the hydrangeas to the convent laundry? When she turned and framed her face in the window and looked right at him, he knew. Almost three years ago. It was Easter week. . . .

HE IS WIDE AWAKE NOW. Where is Margaret? What are those birds? Only chickadees left in November. All that squawking.

It was a night of weeping. Weeping and distance and then violent comings together. Margaret was shattered. Father Paul was stunned, confused, but somehow personally exonerated. That was his mistake. She said he wasn't listening.

He began: "For all his Catholic trappings, all that Irish going back, the French Catholic wife, he was hardly a man of the spirit."

"Enough," said Margaret.

"He was a man of the body, of the secular mind. You know, his father ran liquor."

"You. Envied. Him." She said it evenly, three dead taps.

Father Paul paused, encouraged at the line of conversation. They were on the bed, not in it. Oh, touching was irrelevant. But he'd been rebuked. He liked that. His heartbeat walloped ahead; he could feel his Irish coming up, which made him smart.

"I don't *now*."

Ha-ha. He could only hope a smirk did not sneak out and mar his simple wisdom. Margaret fled to the bathroom, which, weirdly, had the room number on the door, and one of the ones popped off when she slammed it.

THE LIGHT IS GRIM AND GRAY IN ROOM II. He cannot look at his Bulova curled on the nightstand, but he knows it is 7:00 A.M.— an instinct of the seminary—all the hours lived fully in faith and most, alarmingly, in wakefulness. He knows all the hours and the accompanying light according to the seasons, amen.

At 8:00 A.M.—today—he should be saying Mass for Mrs.
Letorneau and Cubby Waldron and the widow Ashline, with
Sister Mary Margaret and the Forkey boys serving. But that
does not seem possible today. It is 7:05 as he coils his Bulova
onto his wrist, where the band snaps, punishing his hairs.
Day begins. It's an hour and a half over the mountain. Call
Mike Seeney. The rector will handle the simple posting.
"Father out on sick call."

Father Paul eyes the cooler. Acrobatically, he retrieves his
socks from just under the night table and slips them on. So
girded, he trods the cold planks and flips the red top up. He
thanks the grace of luck that won the church this fine item
at the Lucky 7 booth at the last picnic. Father Paul'd placed a
dime on number 3 ("for the Trinity," he told the booth worker,
Checkie Farrell, and the assembled). Inside, a single can of
Ballantine ale swims, green and gold, rim nosing above the
surface. Save me; I'm drowning. The sign of the three rings,
Mel Allen. Father lets it drip over the open maw before applying his very own church key, popping a triangular mouth in
the top of the can. He licks the bitter foam, and then fairly
much drains the can. "Crisp," he intones. He wishes it were
beer in the chalice, not being a man for the grape.

He begins to take a spiritual inventory, his examen, as he
often did before breaking fast. Good Jesuit. Of late, it had
been a grim duty, often as not a recounting of the previous
day's iniquity, as now. He was grateful last evening that the
innkeeper had room at the inn. There was indeed a retreat
going on; he was late—and not registered, but who doesn't
trust a priest, even if pulling in quite late in the old Packard
with a nun in the backseat. He lied to Margaret, telling her
he'd lied to the innkeeper, Clem Fessette, saying Sister had
an illness. He pulled around to the back with her out of sight

of the office and knew which room to ask for. In darkness, they had slipped in. His satchel had sufficient things for them both. He always carried them, garments of his faith.

He could deal with this. He'd become hardened to his own sin. He remained in service to his parishioners, their small lives, their small joys, their heartbreaks, marriages, deaths, foibles, sins relayed to him through the screen. He dispensed their penance. They worked their faith and their doubt through him. No one else did this for them, and for the nonce, he wanted it no other way. He wanted Margaret.

She is not far away. Margaret is quite near, perhaps putting on her habit and scapular. Yes, he will see her, very shortly. The prospect makes his face warm and his groin stir, he is awake now, looking about. He finds his trousers and puts them up and on and yanks his belt.

The bathroom door has been closed for too long. He tries the knob. Locked. He thinks he hears her. Yes, he does; that's her. She is sitting on the Eljer toilet, her feet, with their delicate white toes and pale pearl nails, splayed across the soft nap of the floor mat that surrounds the throat of the bowl. Margaret, he thinks to say, but thinks better. Leave her be.

AS HE TRAIPSES IN THE COLD DOWN BELOW the car park to the dark woods near the lakefront, looking for a tree, he rues the fact that he is not the word artist he wanted to be. Sermons are not in his wheelhouse. He knows that. Wasn't *Portrait* the thing that near enlightened him to his calling? It worked on Merton.

Ah, there.

Last year, *The Moviegoer*. Won the big prize. Father Paul read it, but he was no Binx Bolling. He had no desire to hobo

around in search of faith or a good thrashing. *Not* Catholic!
This year a book about priests (there on his nightstand). This,
then, again, this, yes, his fallenness the stuff of art, religious
art, depictions of the struggle for faith. Saint Augustine.

There is hardly any snow for late November, only little
gray stoles of it flung in the gullies. He holds himself a long
time at the base of a birch, his yellow cascading down in
a steaming review. Himself there, but not himself. Pain-
less anyway. Then a shiver of pleasure, and the vapors of
life gently court him, not just his own smells, but also the
dry tang of foliage, the cool musk of damp bark, and the
wind up from the lake carrying a little of the water's residual
summer warmth along with an odor of dead fish. He notes
the sounds around him, too: tree branches creaking, turning in the wind, strengthening themselves; an odd cracking
sound now and then; and, distantly, traffic, out on Route 9,
approaching slowly, gears, then receding into a pinpoint of
silence. Then he hears a cheap door click shut and he knows
he is too late.

There he sees it: the right arm of Mike Seeney extended
and his palm pressing down Margaret's head out of sight as
Seeney's Rambler guns out of the Inn of the Nations parking
lot. Father Paul listens to the gears shifting, first, and straining, second, more straining, third now and cruising, as things
moving away from you will, out of earshot. Deafening.

NOTHING BUT A FUNERAL ON TV—what kind of nation kills
its leader? Lying in state. On both channels, that's all. And
there's Father Hartke, old Gil, the show-biz priest, greeting
people. Father Paul remembers him—a weekend in Mary-
land (conveniently, he was down there for the Preakness, and

Hartke treated). He caught Hartke's Catholic U players the next afternoon. Helen Hayes was there.

What kind of faith kills its savior?

Father Paul Connolly, lying in state, room 11, should anyone care to view the deceased. Clem Fessette must've placed a call to the rectory and Mike Seeney was dispatched to rescue, for once (the word on Mike Seeney: He'll bury you). O my Jesus. The Mass must go on.

Margaret *had* been in the bathroom, then.

Father Paul sees that dear Margaret had had the kindness to make (quickly) the bed. There, hidden in the nightstand drawer behind Gideon, are their ankle belts. Exquisite shackles. Would not fit his neck.

Of course, it had to be Seeney. Margaret had a crush on Mike, like all the sisters. The safe man, celibate now, a widower, childless, devoted to the church and grounds. More pious than he. The man who hand-dug all the graves and buried the dead of the parish. He did his work softly and soundlessly, as if in a silent film, hardly disturbing the surface of the earth for his interments. Hadn't Father Paul seen Seeney blush at the church picnic in August, when a small dribble of Michigan sauce slipped down his chin and Margaret wiped it away with her finger. She smiled in such a warm way that Mike had to fetch something from the shed.

Not very hygienic, for an Ursuline, Sister, said her pastor.

Father, she whispered. He who is clean among us . . .

That kind of brash he both loved and feared. But now, of course, he had other things to fear. Seeney had spied the pastor's Packard, if not the strewn bedsheets in the room. Margaret's tears in the car (inevitable), her damp lashes and sniffles, could have as cover the death of the president, if she wished it to. *If.* Conversely, she could be destroying Father Paul right now in Seeney's Rambler somewhere on Route 22. Right around Peru, the dead orchards.

Noon. And why had it come to this? Father Paul was sitting up in bed. No more Ballantines in the cooler. All of college football canceled or preempted, just like Father Paul—at this point, he was simply a test pattern—a big silent Indian chief, with no tribe. But it had come to this and Margaret had warned him, warned him that his lack of piety, his weakness, his harsh judgments of his fellow man, were fatiguing her, weakening her in faith and body, and he was slipping beyond her capacity to hold on to him. Especially in the face of her own "contradictions," as she called them. Ah, but she'd never consign him to the fire.

She was leaving the Church herself, she said. He could not, and would not, and would she without him? And she would not! This is what he had wanted to talk about during the night, not the unimaginable events in Dallas—the horror of it. The sudden death of a prince. The weeping.

He sought a confessor.

"CLEM," HE SAYS, OPENING THE DOOR next to the sign that said OFFICE. "Do you have anything I might eat?"

"Father, shouldn't you be getting back?" Father Paul can hear the solemn notes of the broadcast beneath Clem's counter somewhere, the click of shoes in the East Room of the White House, the sighing of veils and men.

"Clem, I should not. I am not well today. A curate from St. Alex's is covering," he says, lying.

"Nothing for you to eat, Father. The missus isn't bringing over my dinner today. She's watching this and you can't talk to her. I should be home, but for this retreat going on."

"It's an empty parking lot, Clem."

Clem just looks at Father Paul, his only guest.

"You should be getting back. I can give you a drink," says Clem. He produces a bottle of VO from beneath the counter. "There's 7 Up and Coke and Fanta in the machine. Ice-cold."

Father Paul, surprising himself, declines, but does ring up a Coke bottle, which dropped out of the big red machine like ordnance. The bleakness of it—man and soda, November afternoon.

"Ice-cold all right," he says, palming it. "Thanks, Clem. Bless you."

Halfway through the door, Father Paul turns. "Clem, Inn of the Nations. What nations?" But Clem has retired to the back.

OH, IT IS OVER. Father Paul stands in his room and looks out the window. He can see nothing but sky, gray and featureless. Rampant, he thinks, as in spreading, unchecked. A good word, that. And the vacuum of his future—his rampant future, spreading, unchecked? Hardly. There's no one in it, out there only vanished souls—his mother's, his father's, and wherever Sarah's is. Now Margaret, off with Mike Seeney. And nowhere his faith, his Holy God, his service, his sanctity. The Coca-Cola revived him some.

Not rampant. Contracting.

Sitting in a chair, TV off, he opens the curtains. Come on in, he says, inviting the cold scrutiny of midafternoon. He settles in with his book, the condemned man's last cigarette.

Ironic: a priest novel. He recalls that the book won the big award (lot's of to-do: The monsignor mentioned it in his bulletin), and Father Paul'd committed the sin of envy. Was the author a priest? He was not, apparently, from the back flap—J.F. Powers, "raised in a devout family," a CO in the war—good for him. But: Father Urban? What's that make him, Father Rural?

Made quite a stir, anyway. Beat out the Russian with the nymphet. Ha! A good time for the Catholics right now (till yesterday). But what to learn?

Father Paul, since falling ass over teakettle for Margaret three years ago, hadn't written a word in his "Soul Journey," his work in progress, fashioned after *The Spiritual Exercises*, which instruction, he has thought more than once, was to find a kind of engagement with belief and discipline and spiritual cleansing that a small French girl had delivered in a single afternoon.

As a Jesuit, of course, Ignatius's *Exercises*, the four-week regimen of spiritual examen, was a rite of passage. All struggled with it, but Paul Connolly, self-trained in ardent visualization of the scriptural, shined. As he sat in the pale seepage of the one window to Room 11, he recited the Fifth Exercise, a meditation on hell: "The first Point will be to see with the sight of the imagination the great fires, and the souls as in bodies of fire. The second, to hear with the ears wailings, howlings, cries, blasphemies against Christ our Lord and against all His Saints. The third, to smell with the smell smoke, sulphur, dregs and putrid things. The fourth, to taste with the taste bitter things, like tears, sadness and the worm of conscience. The fifth, to touch with the touch—" But he could not go on.

Yes, he should be visualizing his own torment right now— Hell, his hell; wailings, howlings, cries, blasphemies against Christ our Lord, his rantings; smoke and dregs and putrid things, here in room 11; the awful taste of tears, the worm of conscience—the worm! His. And the touch of fire—on his skin. But no, he is thumbing through a piece of fiction.

He could be visualizing the torment of a widow and a family and a nation right now—his vocation, look at Hartke—but he is not. This is a tragedy that *shall not be read.*

What is transpiring in his life is a tragedy, too—that *shall not be read.*

It won't even be written.

The Book of the Month people—it takes him a while to figure this out—are offering a short story by the author as a little appetizer.

As he begins the story—"The Presence of Grace"—he flinches at the *absence* of it, and of Margaret, and of his vocation, all fled. The presence of emptiness yawns around him in the silent landscape of a splattered world. He's got the TV on now, for atmosphere. Funerary art. He is remains. Of the dead. He has been cast adrift in another dimension, from which he can see the world spinning away into its intricately charged orbits, while he will tumble slowly through space alone.

Father Paul cannot write. He cannot even think . . . of . . . the empty rectory, the loneliness or anger of Margaret, perhaps hatred, perhaps pain of confusion. No. Mike Seeney ministering her—minister!—or the gaggle of sisters gossiping. He won't even merit a search party, will he? He matters not. He digs into the text—the consolations of prose. The oblivion of other people's words.

For the next two hours Father Paul follows one Father Fabre, a curate to a daft pastor who is stubbornly antisocial (likes to picnic by himself, go to the zoo, and count the collections in his room—by himself). Fabre tries to compensate, balancing out the parish presence by accepting invitations to dinner from parishioners, only to make a grave mistake: He becomes coerced into offering his blessing to an unmarried older couple living together, in sin, of course, while the curate for the duration of the meal is paired with a young single woman, who tells him, "I know priests who are married." Father Fabre escapes, but he understands what he has done. He bravely presents his dilemma to the pastor, who, it is immediately clear, will have to intervene with a council of outraged parishioners who want him to do something about his wayward curate and the sinning couple. But the old guy just refuses to accept their account that anything untoward has happened and manages to do it in a way that does not offend them, or accuse them of misrepresenting the facts. " 'S not so," he simply tells them, and nothing more. " 'S not so."

Father Paul finds himself laughing throughout this tale at the author's gentle sarcasm delivered in sentences as sharp as strung diamonds, all facets beautifully balanced in the weight of clauses and the light they carry. As the offending older gentleman, the wonderfully named (and diminutive) Mr. Pint, struggles in the summer heat to turn the ice-cream crank, Father Fabre quietly offers to take a turn. "But Mr. Pint, out to deny his size and years, needed no help, or lost in his exertions, had not heard."

Father Paul laughs loudly, and rereads the lines about Mr. Pint—such care and attention and not a little bit of dignity bestowed upon the little man's efforts through the writer's own. Father Paul reads around in the story, delight after delight. When he reaches the end, where, indeed, there is a near-miraculous presence of grace in the church—the pastor's way, gentle stonewalling, perhaps the Church's way, prevails—Father Paul feels joy in his breast, at last: All come together to pray before the curate at devotions; his pastor, in the "dim, dell-like recesses of the nave," opens a few windows. A lovely feat, a lovely, perfect story, and Father Paul begins to whimper then, to feel his eyes moisten, perhaps a cry coming. Somehow, he understands what it is to listen. The Lord listens.

There is a knock on the door to room 11. "It's Mike, Father. You must open up."

Seeney, his face worn, stands there, with state troopers at his shoulders—like crows, thinks Father Paul.

The Newman Boys

—

I

"Clean underwear, Michael," said Michael's mother when she knocked on his door in the morning. He knew what this meant: They were going clothes shopping.

Michael's mother had directed his back-to-school shopping the previous August, on the eve of his entrance into seventh grade. It was considered a success. When outfitted, he looked neither like a farmer nor a beatnik, but "a young man from Andover," as his mother put it. Michael didn't know what to think. But that was last year, an okay school year, in his view. He'd made the honor roll; he'd finished third in the low hurdles at Field Day and received a ribbon; and, at the end of the school year, he'd proven himself adept at spin the bottle. In the last six months or so, he'd had his growth spurt—he was no longer a size 14 boys'. He might even be a men's small.

It was big news for Michael's mother to drive the Cadillac *anywhere*. In her worldview, women didn't drive; they were driven—in every sense of the word. Michael didn't know if this made his mother modern or old-fashioned, and he didn't know whom to ask.

The everyday driving in the family was left mostly to his father, who motored the old Ford truck with the emblem of a

big bull on the driver's side door to and from the barn twice
a day, ran errands, and made his Friday-night jaunts to the
taverns on the river, where he talked local politics, shot pool,
and came back with a few stories that he shared carefully at
Saturday supper. And then there was the handyman, Ted Farrell, who drove a little. Ted helped on the farm some but was
generally at the beck and call of Michael's mother. It was Ted
who squired her to her hair appointments, to checkups with
Dr. Forquet, and for her monthly visit to the credit union in
Dannemora to make her deposits.

Indeed, Gwendolyn (Chilcott) Touhey spent most of her
time right at home in the large salon, doing her accounts—
Michael understood that a block of properties she'd inherited
in Troy was the principle source of the family income. The
Touheys lived in the biggest house in town, a three-story Vic-
torian with a widow's walk and a cupola, though they were
the smallest family in Oreville, but for the childless.

IT HAD BEEN A SULLEN SUMMER for Michael. A yellow coin
of impetigo on his right shin had kept him from the swimming hole during most of August, and a badly sprained left
ankle, incurred in the spring while playing in the hayloft, had
dashed most of his Little League season. To make matters
worse, in July his best friend's family had moved away, taking
his best friend's older sister, Pearl, with them. Michael, as a
result of these deprivations, spent most of his spare time during that summer of '66 reading the *Sporting News* his father
would bring home, with its endless statistics on every major-
league team as well as stats on all the minor leagues—the
Pacific Coast League, the International League, the American
Association, all the way down to the rookie leagues. It was

Michael's world. And there was also the one old copy of *Playboy* he'd stolen from the outhouse at Macomb Park: Stella Stevens stretched out on a white mink bench, plus a long, confounding story by Ernest Hemingway. Michael's next world. As Labor Day weekend approached, for the first time he found himself adrift and, also for the first time, excited about returning to school. He was looking forward to the trip with his mother to find a new wardrobe.

"It's the finest men's clothier south of Montreal," his mother said at breakfast—a soft-boiled egg in a cup, three fingers of toast for her, a bowl of Wheaties and glass of prune juice for him. "The finest north of Bergdorf's. The Merkels are Jewish, you know.

"Now wash up."

THE FIFTEEN-MILE TRIP TO THE NEAREST CITY, where there were nice shops in an actual downtown with traffic lights and metered parking and a pizza parlor, was very navigable; indeed, it was a leisurely route—a well-banked two-lane road that followed the easy laze of the river. Michael's mother drove slowly, with no distractions—no radio, no conversation. She eyed the road with an intense concentration. She shared this with her son, catching her breath at a four-way stop: "You line up the hood ornament with the stripe on the right shoulder and you'll always know where you are."

She wore hose with that thick black line down the back of each calf like an angry vein. She wore heels, making her taller than her son, who was in khakis and tennis shoes and a light jacket over a sweatshirt. As she strode down the aisle of Merkel's, greetings of "Mrs. Touhey, good day to you" came from two men on the floor. Michael walked in her wake.

Michael knew he was the only boy from Oreville, a poor town, to be shopping at Merkel's—aside from Norton & Sons, it was the most expensive around. The Merkels' shop—long and narrow and high-ceilinged—featured chocolaty cherrywood shelving and cabinets. You could open a little glass door on sweet hinges and look at ties, or you could gently tug a drawer that slowly rolled toward you with a pleasing rattle and inspect the folded shirts there arrayed. It was as if everything had already found a home and was in its place, and you were just there viewing someone's magnificent personal collection. But it was all for sale.

A grid of pigeonholes, like something you might see behind the desk at a hotel on a TV show, held plush cotton socks, each pair folded in half so that what you saw was a soft turn of color—blues on blacks on grays on greens—stacked in long columns. On the higher shelves, above offerings of men's colognes standing on a marble mantel, were the sweaters—V-necks, crews, cardigans, turtlenecks.

"The cornflower is nice," Michael's mother said. "Goes with your eyes. But I'll leave you alone. I'll pop into Norton's next door. I need a hat."

Through several costume changes in the fitting room, Michael tried to imagine himself in different guises. But since he was concentrating on how he might look to Jody Favaro, in his class, or the incoming Sandy Champaigne, who already had a reputation, his choices were fairly narrow: Those girls were both from Morrisonville, how different could they be? He looked at himself in the full-length mirror. He looked at himself as he was—a dopey kid in Nowheresville. He wanted to look like George Harrison. He wanted a long, lean face with sunken cheeks and high cheekbones and big teeth. He wanted a face that was sad and witty; that would do. But he looked like Opie Taylor—no glamour, no forelock. He couldn't wait till he had to shave.

After an hour or so, his mother came calling. She seemed rushed and excited, in high color. She was rocking one toe up on a high heel. Michael was glumly looking through a glass-topped cabinet—at tie pins and men's grooming implements. He wished for the future. He wanted to go home but could never say so in words. She didn't ask what had happened. It was up to him to say. And nothing had happened. He looked at her as if to say, So?

Michael's mother spoke rapidly and spun two parallel streams of content. First, that she had found, next door "just the style for you—more Continental, shall we say. Come see." And that she had run into Mrs. Newman there—"of the Newman family moving into the Dashnaw house."

The Dashnaw house was where Michael had spent much of his childhood—it was where his friend Terry Dashnaw lived, had lived, and where Terry's older sister, Pearl, had lived, and grown, and ditched Bucky Weir because of what happened at the keg party, and slept, in that bedroom Michael could see from his own, where when her light went out, so did his. Perhaps she'd notice. But now it didn't matter. They'd moved.

"Come, let's go next door to Norton's."

Norton's was a traditional English shop, always out of fashion except to the few folks in the area—college deans and surgeons and such—who might fancy custom shirts or have need of a boot maker. But Michael's mother, perhaps correctly, had connected the staid British style to what the new music bands from England were wearing.

Michael's mother had an odd respect for the Beatles. As a family, they had watched the band's ballyhooed appearance on *The Ed Sullivan Show* two years before. Everything was dark, a snowed-in winter Sunday night. Not long after the president had been killed and the Catholic priest in town had had a breakdown, these longhaired boys appeared to all that screaming and Michael's mother decided they were polite, well-dressed boys with lovely voices. Michael's father snorted at that but seemed to agree. And Michael thought all the boys seemed strange except George, who was the youngest, still a teenager.

Mother and son walked into Norton & Sons.

WHEN THEY GOT HOME, Michael carried all his packages into his room, where he planned to array them on his bed in private to see just what he had done, but his mother insisted he come to the kitchen table for some lunch. As he helped prepare, working the can opener, setting out "fork, then knife, then spoon," he sensed his mother had something to say. There was something she wanted.

"I know this Mrs. Newman," she said brightly. Now Michael remembered: the new neighbors. "It is the most extraordinary thing, running into her—I had just wandered into Norton's to give you some time to yourself, and there she was! I recognized her as a Farthing, and I introduced myself. I knew her sister, it turns out, Mabel Farthing, at St. Rose. Mabel and I were in the same house. I think I even met her younger sister, this Hilda, during one of the parents' days, oh so long ago. And now she's a neighbor."

Michael didn't know what to make of this. He pressed finger marks into his sandwich, five of them, in a circle. "The Farthings are a very, very good family," said Michael's mother, flapping her napkin square over her lap. "Stop that, Michael. Mabel was a beauty, and she played piano beautifully. The family was in steel, I believe. Mabel married an Aldrich. Hilda told me that she went to Smith."

Michael had to ask what Smith was and was told, but he wondered who else was in this new family. His mother moved quickly to dispense more of the intelligence she'd gleaned on the floor of Norton's.

"You will be delighted to know that they have two boys and one boy is exactly your age." She bit lightly into her sandwich, maintaining a strained smile. "His name is Thomas. He plays the piano. They have a piano. And he will be in your home-room—you do have Jane Davies again, don't you?"

He did have Mrs. Davies. And this certainly was of inter-est to Michael. "The back street," as their road was called, ran for about a mile through the small town. Although the local school was a centralized school, attracting kids from half a dozen surrounding towns whose schools had closed, Oreville itself, in the dead of summer, was just another lit-tle empty hamlet, and having enough boys to get up a ball game was always a challenge. Two more would help. Having a piano was unusual, for Oreville. But maybe that's interest-ing, Michael thought.

"What about the other kid?" he asked.

"A kid is a goat, Michael." She put her sandwich down as if in admonition but then resumed her testimony. "The other boy is two years younger; he's in the lower school, with Liz Canning, fifth grade. And school starts next week, as you well know. But I made an arrangement for you to visit them tomorrow and introduce yourself to the boys. You will do that, won't you ? Of course. After lunch, let's see one of your outfits."

Michael wasn't so sure of his outfits. He wondered what he had done or let happen. English modern fashion—fancy

shirts and "waistcoats," pants that fit tight and pointy
toed boots. Was this a style for northern New York, where
most men farmed or guarded prisoners or cut wood? What
would Sandy Champaigne think? He pressed a finger dot
in the middle of his tuna sandwich and studied its design.
His thinking cut the circle into five identical sectors, each
seventy-two degrees, he reasoned. He was grateful for the
intercession of his father, who came banging in, wearing his
usual work clothes and grin.

"How's Mickey?" he asked. "*Comment ça va?* How's your
crosscut saw, eh?" He rubbed his boy's head with his knuckle,
and swooped to kiss his wife of twenty years, who offered her
left cheek, which Patrick Touhey pecked with merry exaggera-
tion, teasing her reserve, as usual. "Don't be shy, Gwendy," he
said, which, as always, made Michael cringe and his mother
flinch. Patrick Touhey just laughed.

"Mick, what do you say we hop in the truck," he said. His
father had the freezer compartment door open and was fetch-
ing an Eskimo Pie—two, then.

"Okay, Dad."

The ride up the hill was nice. Michael had always liked
it. From the top, he could look back at the valley, and see
the river, and their house standing tall down there, taller
than the trees on the back street. Soft sunshine glazing the
windshield, his father chatting about his Giants and Juan
Marichal. "Tied for first," he said. But Michael didn't follow
the National League much. "With who?" He looked across
his father's shoulder to the settlement on the other side of
the valley, where there were mostly farms and stands of trees
and the one road going over it, to the top. Down the other
side was yet another valley with other small towns. It gave
Michael perspective.

"The Dodgers. It's a pennant race."

"What about the Sox?"—Michael's team, if he had one. He liked Tony C., the youngest home run champ of all time.

"Boston's way out of it," said his father, shouting over the old truck boards rattling loud. "And in the other league."

The cows, all thirteen of them, were kept in the lower part of the barn. His father would buy yearlings for a little money (this is how Michael understood it), then feed them for a couple of years and fatten them up, keep them free of disease, and then sell them for milking cows to one of the dairy farmers along the lake, for good money. A big cow would bring four hundred dollars. Michael understood from his father that it was "a good payday" when it came. He bought his truck with the proceeds a couple of years ago, and bought Gwendolyn a brooch.

The job was to feed them. Mostly, the calves spent their time in their own stanchions. That was the word, and Michael had never heard it outside the farm, but now he knew it. Steel rods running vertically that opened a bit and closed around the calf's neck just behind the ears. They chomped on hay bales they could reach and tumbled turds like knots of rope and gushed urine out their back ends into a running gutter ("Watch your step!"). In the morning, Michael's father would break up the bales for them to eat, and then in the afternoon or early evening, like now, he'd would go up to the barn, pull a lever that opened all the stanchions, and the cattle would back out and mill about like they had no idea what to do.

"It's good for them to walk around, get their legs under 'em," said Michael's father, who had to encourage them to get out into the little pen for some fresh air and to see what the world was like—fields and farm and distant tree lines, same stuff Michael saw, though they seldom raised their heads.

There were several salt blocks on posts out in the pen. What Michael didn't like was this part and the part that followed.

In this year's crop, there was one calf that was a lot smaller, and she couldn't even think about getting to the salt lick— she was butted out of the way as soon as she approached, not big enough to get a lick in. And the next part, after Michael's father herded the calves into the barn with a few "heps" and waving of his straw hat, was worse, when in a big barrel his father mixed a kind of powder and water—"enriched," his father said—and the battle for gobbling the paste was even more fierce and the little one just stood off to the side in surrender. Michael felt sorry for the little thing.

"Dad, what about the little one?" Michael often asked this. He prided himself on the times he didn't.

"Don't worry about the mooley," said his father, who watched the frenzy at the barrel for a while. In about five minutes, when the other dozen had fed enough in his view, he cleared a path and escorted the mooley to the barrel by the scruff of its neck and there added a little mix with a tin scoop for the mooley's private meal. "Needs the nourishment," he said. "She'll be too small to sell. She'll end up your pet."

"I don't want a cow for a pet, Dad." His father winked at him, the paste lathered up his forearms like long white gloves. And the mooley looked at Michael with one big eye of alarm.

THAT NIGHT AT HOME, suddenly, Michael was the entertainment. After supper and the evening news, his father called for "a fashion show." Michael thought this was a joke at first, or that perhaps *The Liberace Show* was coming on—his father's voice had that edge. But no, and his mother went along.

"Let's see your new duds," his father said. "Turn the TV off."

"Yes, let's," said his mother.

Michael trudged to his bedroom. He'd already laid out everything he and his mother had bought, across his (this really had to go) chenille cowboy bedspread: four shirts, including two paisley numbers and one with a ruffle; four narrow pairs of trousers that already looked too short for him; a short jacket with a wide lapel like a munchkin's; and those leather boots—with heels. His face was hot.

He walked out to the living room, and his mother said, "Want some help?"

"I wanna die," he said, appealing to his father, who gave a quick shake of his head, like it was a punch line to a joke he'd missed. His father said, "What?"

"Michael, now," said his mother, rising. "Transitions are difficult. You looked very sharp in the shop."

"I'll look like an idiot!"

His father got up and left.

His mother, casting a disapproving glance at the space her husband had left, counseled patience. "Michael, you're tired. Give it some time. It's a new year and it should be a new you, in every way." She went over to him and gave him a rare hug, and pinched his fiery cheek. "You're warm, Michael." His chance.

Feigning fever, Michael went to his room—moving everything off the bed onto the floor of his closet. He undressed, tuned the radio to a station far away. He heard his father back the truck out, bound for the tavern, no doubt. His mother, he could hear, made her phone calls.

THE LAST MOVING VAN HAD LEFT the Dashnaw place. Michael had tried not to watch as the items left behind by the Dashnaws, including the old sprung convertible couch he himself had slept on, were trundled out. An entire family's stuff had been moved in—large cabinets and dressers, dozens of boxes, and then the delicate on-its-side entrance of what must be the piano, wrapped in a white sheet. No sign of the boys, only what looked like Mr. Newman, a tall man wearing a hat, directing things and at times putting a shoulder to the effort. By Friday evening, all the lights were on in the two-story house Michael knew so well, just like when the Dashnaws were there on any Friday night. Michael had what he thought was a very adult thought: I'm too young for nostalgia.

"They're all in," Michael's mother asserted, looking out their picture window at the lit-up house. "You can visit in the morning."

Michael Touhey was in possession of the bulk of the sports equipment at his end of the back street. Some kids didn't have mitts or decent balls or a selection of bats. No one else, in fact, had a real leather football, just plastic things that floated unpredictably and were more like bath toys. So Michael, who was excited to meet the two Newman kids, put three mitts—his brand-new one and two he had outgrown—in his bike basket, and tossed in a hardball, a softball, and a Wiffle ball. Just as he was ready to go, his mother came out with a wrapped loaf pan. "Banana bread for Mrs. Newman," she said. "A housewarming gift."

When he got up to the house, he leaned his bike against the front porch railing as he always had, and put the baseball mitts on the porch, where the boys or Mr. or Mrs. Newman, when they came out, if they came out, would see them. He carried the banana bread in the crook of his arm like a football. When he got to the door, he realized that, unlike in the Dashnaw days, he'd better knock.

Through the screen, he saw Mr. and Mrs. Newman already standing, both of them tall and young-looking, younger than his own parents. They could be TV parents, like the Cleavers. They looked efficient. Mr. Newman had a tie on. Mrs. Newman wore a flowered apron over her dress, and had earrings on and lipstick. She wore cat's-eye glasses with a kind of chain that went around her neck, beneath her hair. She was pretty.

"You must be Michael," said Mrs. Newman, pushing the door open. "Can this be Michael?" said Mr. Newman, extending his hand, his left hand. He had a big gold watch. His right sleeve—his right arm—was missing.

Michael shook his hand awkwardly, but it was a nicer, warmer handshake than the normal kind. He said hello as best he could and caught himself walking into the familiar hallway.

"Oh, here," he said, turning, stopping. "From my mother. It's banana bread."

Mrs. Newman made a delighted fuss and took it from him. "My!" she said.

"Mmm," said Mr. Newman, leaning in a bit to smell. "Do you prefer Mike or Michael?" he asked, patiently waiting for an answer to a question that Michael had never heard.

"I don't know," he said. "Michael."

"Boys," Mrs. Newman announced. "A new friend is here!"

At the foot of the stairs, Michael waited. He could hear footsteps above. He wondered which one had Terry's room and which one had Pearl's. What he figured was the little one headed down first, the sounds of skipping and whistling. He jumped with a thud to the landing above—he had new Keds on—and then took the last three steps in another leap and landed right at Michael's feet.

"Hey!"

"Phillip, this is Michael Touhey, from down the hill. He goes to your school. Or I should say, you go to his." She winked at Michael. She was nice.

Michael said hi. He could see that the little kid thought the name Touhey sounded funny, although he didn't say anything. Good. Michael wanted to get outdoors or go farther inside, but there were slow footsteps still descending. The older boy's tread sounded as if he were carrying something. Indeed, when a figure arrived at the first landing, Michael saw an unsteady step—new Keds, too. Everyone—Phillip, his parents, and Michael—were looking expectantly. And the boy—"Here's Tommy now," said his mother—turned the corner, carrying something on his shoulder, like maybe a ball, Michael thought, one of those big, soft yellow kick balls, when Michael realized it was the boy's head.

The little hallway was suddenly cramped and warm, and Mr. Newman opened the screen door and everyone trooped out. Michael was invited to exit first and the others followed. Michael looked off the porch, across the road, into the big oak tree that had one patch going lightly orange, and he wished he were there. His scalp needled and his thoughts weren't his own. He took a deep breath. When he turned around, the new family in town was before him, like a strange cartoon. The slender poles of parents, the little cute boy, and the boy with the head shaped like balloon listing to the side, as if it was losing air. The boy—Tommy—seemed to strain to keep it where it was, which wasn't straight. It looked like he, or it, his head, might fall to the porch. But he was grinning, looking down at the porch, where the three baseball mitts were.

"Have a catch, boys," said Mr. Newman. "Michael seems to've brought plenty of equipment." Turning directly to

Michael, Mr. Newman confided that he boys' own baseball gear was still in boxes. They all went down the two steps to the front yard, then to the side of the house, the little one, Phillip, skipping ahead, with a glove on his left hand and tossing a ball up with his right and staggering around underneath to catch it. Tommy, moving more slowly, had his glove on—that is, Michael's current glove, the Willie Mays MacGregor model—and seemed to know what to do with it, but then he sat down on the grass. Michael didn't know what to do. He picked up his old glove. Then he went over to Tommy and handed him the hardball. "That glove needs some breaking in. Pound it a bit."

And Tommy popped the ball into the pocket—*whap, whap, whap, whap.* And Michael played catch—at a little distance—with the smaller boy. Mr. and Mrs. Newman retreated to the porch and watched, Mr. Newman's one arm around Mrs. Newman.

They continued like this for a while. The parents went inside after advising their boys not to wander off and asking Michael if perhaps he would show them a few things. "It's his town," Mrs. Newman said, smiling at Michael, who was pleased to think of it that way.

Michael showed them the sand pit where he used to play army men with Terry Dashnaw. He showed them where the brook ran out back. Michael was confused about Tommy's head, but, other than the fact that Tommy moved slowly, his large skull drifting like a cloud above him, they were just three normal kids. The Newman boys were okay, he decided. The little one was funny and had crazy things in his pockets, like a little door hinge, a tiny flashlight, and a rubber worm. Tommy spoke quietly. He said he liked animals. Michael asked him what his favorite animal was. "Ungulates," Tommy said, helpfully adding, "they sustain their entire body weight on their toes. Like zebras and hippos." Michael noticed as he listened that all Tommy's features were at a slant.

Michael asked where they were from. Tommy said Slingerlands. He said his father was going to teach at the mental hospital in Dannemora. "He's a psychologist," he said.

The boys stood for quite a while playing in the brook and looking at it. Michael showed them the wide, flat rock where you could get down and drink from the brook. He demonstrated. Phillip flopped right down and slurped the water. "Cold!" he declared. Tommy declined.

When they went back to the house, Mrs. Newman had slices of banana bread on plates for them at the big dining room table they had set up in what used to be the Dashnaws' living room. The boys sat down and she poured them each a tall glass of milk.

The boys ate in silence. Michael wanted to go home. But Mrs. Newman said, "Tommy, will you play something? Dad is just finishing leveling the piano. Aren't you, dear?" she yelled in a way that seemed teasing, like maybe he'd been at it awhile.

Tommy rose and went to the little room that Michael remembered as a messy laundry when the Dashnaws were there. It now had plants, and bright, clean windows, and a shiny black upright piano. They all entered—the boys, that is, and Mrs. Newman. Mr. Newman was already there, on his knees, working a small tool under the piano. He removed a wedge of wood and said, "Piece of cake," winking at Mrs. Newman, as if maybe he was kidding.

When Michael looked behind him, there were four or five folding chairs along the wall, and they all sat down. Tommy maneuvered onto the piano bench, lifted the cover, and seemed to think for a moment.

Then he played a song that Michael immediately recognized from his mother's collection of sound tracks, which she would play every once in a while. Michael used to put the needle to this one himself sometimes, for just this song. He liked to look at the album cover, too, because it was a musical about baseball and had a long-legged lady in underwear on the front.

Phillip belted out the chorus. By the time Tommy reached the end, they were all singing.

"Damned Yankees," Mr. Newman said when it was over. "Are you a Yankee fan?" he asked Michael. Michael definitely wasn't that. "No!" he said. And then he surprised himself, "I've got miles of heart!"

"So do we," said Mr. Newman, looking warmly at his boys and at Michael in their chairs. "Red Sox fans."

OVER A RARE ITALIAN SPAGHETTI SUPPER, Michael's parents were eager to know about his visit, what the house and the people and the Newman boys were like.

Michael began by talking about the older boy's piano playing, but his father cut him off. "Start at the beginning. Did you meet the Newmans?"

"You mean the parents?"

"Yeah, boy, I mean the parents."

"The father's got one arm."

"Yeah, I heard," said his father, shaking from a green can grated Parmesan onto his spaghetti.

"You did?" said Michael's mother.

"Go on, Mick," said Michael's father.

"Well, they have a real nice piano."

"Yeah, we saw it, didn't we, moving in there. And you heard that—Gwendy, didn't the lady tell you, 'Oh, we have a piano'? Yeah, we know that. What else?"

"Patrick," Michael's mother said. "Don't be cross."

"Cross? I just want to know what our boy thinks of his new neighbors."

"Well," said Michael. "The fifth grader is a nice kid—I can't remember his name! Phillip! That's it. The older boy, Tommy . . . is a little, different. He's got something that might be wrong with him. But he's nice."

"What's that? What's that 'something might be wrong with him' thing?" said Michael's father, deliberately, as if he were stepping over stones in a stream, which signaled to Michael that something was up, like perhaps the drinking thing was a problem again.

"Tommy has a . . . large . . . head," said Michael.

"Yeah-yeah-yeah-yeah," said his father, finally digging into his spaghetti, the signal that everyone else could. "I heard there was a goddamned carnival show up there."

Michael's mother twirled pasta onto her fork with the assist of her big spoon, and kept twirling it, and said nothing and looked at no one.

GOT UP IN WHAT HE FELT was the least aggressive outfit—the quieter paisley and the black trousers—Michael left early for his first day of school. He'd admit he didn't want to end up walking into the building with the Newman boys. It was hard enough dealing with his own new look. He walked by himself in sharp-pointed, shiny boots past the cowpats at the mouth of Larry Weldon's driveway and past Downey's scrawny little apple orchard and then the gas station, where the brook crossed under the road, before he got to the school parking lot and made the last endless one hundred yards in full view of anyone already at the school who cared to look through the glass doors. He'd made it. In the main hallway, he was greeted by Mr. Kenneally, the mean principal with the permanent five o'clock shadow, who was all smiles today and didn't give Michael any trouble or teasing. Michael spent a little time looking at the trophy cases but really checking out just how out of place he looked amid the gleam of sports team memorabilia, and then he saw them, behind him: Mrs. and Mrs. Newman, Phillip and Tommy flanking, and the guidance counselor's secretary, Miss Dubray, and the school nurse, Miss Gregoire, hovering.

"Michael," said Miss Gregoire. "Will you show Tommy to your homeroom? You're both with Mrs. Davies. You know where that is."

Tommy looked pretty good in his denim outfit, pants and jean jacket, along with a white-collared soft cotton shirt and desert boots. Still, his head lolled like a slow fish in the sea and he'd see you with first one eye and then the other.

Mrs. and Mrs. Newman didn't make a big thing of saying good-bye, but instead followed Miss Dubray, who escorted Phillip to Mrs. Canning's room.

Michael and Tommy made their way down the staircase to the lower level. At the bottom—of course!—Jody Favaro and two other girls. The three of them were ready to say hello, but when Jody got a look at Tommy, she burst into a laugh, almost like a shout. Two fingers of yellow snot slipped down her upper lip till she sucked them back up with a snort. Mortified! That was the new Sandy Champaigne she was with, all dark and cool and bored-looking. Jody went flailing off to the girl's room, shrieking, "Freak!"

"Who's the freak," Michael heard Sandy Champagne mutter in disgust, not really a question, walking in the opposite direction, indicting all. She had a cigarette behind her ear and was headed out the side door. "Some outfit, guy." A comment meant for Michael. He didn't know what to make of it.

The next day, Michael, with the help of his mother and the nurse—Miss Gregoire had called Mrs. Touhey and they met in the nurse's office—was able to understand what hydrocephalus was—called "water on the brain," it was actually an excess of spinal fluid spilling into the skull. There were kinds of treatments—and Tommy had already had some—where they drained the fluid out of his head into his stomach. Michael asked if Tommy was going to die, and his mother reminded him that everyone dies, and Miss Gregoire added that Tommy might not live as long a life as Michael but that he could lead a good life. "And that's what we all want."

That might've been all they wanted, but as the year got under way, it was awful for Tommy. His second day, there was a Mr. Potato Head sitting on his homeroom desk. When he got to study hall, there was a Mr. Potato Head drawn on the blackboard. In the second week, at recess, Dickie Trudeau had a big inflatable ball that he'd drawn a face on and they batted it around the school yard, yelling, "Come here, Newman!"

Michael was so upset by the whole thing, he became mean. He put all his new clothes back in their boxes and stashed them in the closet, even if Sandy Champaigne (maybe) thought they were cool. He told his mother he was wearing blue jeans till the British style came into fashion in Oreville. "We're behind the times," he told her, and she seemed to agree. His father was no help, just staying on the sidelines, as if something he had long understood was just dawning on the rest of mankind.

MICHAEL BECAME TROUBLED, in those early weeks of eighth grade, with the unfairness of everything. The things he didn't understand—why the Dashnaws had moved away, why girls everywhere were screaming for the Beatles but not here, why the mooley got abused and starved by his own kind, and why his schoolmates were so cruel to Tommy Newman. Or why his big house had a mother always busy with her accounts and a father who seemed like he had no purpose in the world other than feeding cows or playing cards and dressing in the same clothes every day. Michael decided not to try out for the basketball team. He also decided not to go to the football games on Saturdays.

Michael was moping around the house one brilliant autumn Saturday when his father, blowing into the house with a leaf in his hair, said that he should get down to the school. "Playing Beekmantown, big game," he said. Michael remained silent. His mother was at the kitchen counter, preparing yet another pot of tea. "Why don't you go up and see the Newman boys. Maybe they'd like to go," she said.

"The boy can go on his own," barked his father as he left through the back door.

His mother, to Michael's surprise, had absorbed the afflictions of the new neighbors in stride. She talked to Mrs. Newman on the phone with some regularity. Though she took the calls at her desk, out of earshot, it was clear she thought the world of Mrs. Newman, who, she reported, had graduated magna cum laude and had been to Paris, and Mr. Newman who, she reminded all, was Doctor Newman, not mister. Michael's father was not charmed by any of it. "If Newman calls himself a shrink, I can think of one thing he should—"

"Patrick! I will not hear that again," Michael's mother said, cutting him off.

"Root, root, root for the home team," his father sang in taunting singsong from the backyard while aggressively raking the ground for leaves.

Michael said to himself, "He's pissing me off." Michael got up, grabbed his football, ran through the backyard. Just to fool his father.

"Attaboy."

Michael didn't turn right toward the school and the football game, but walked straight up the hill to visit the Newman boys. He knew they wouldn't be going to the game, at least not Tommy, as he'd been sick the last week or so, spending time in the nurse's office with headaches, till his mother came to take him home.

"Tommy's sitting up in bed, but he'd love to see you," said Mrs. Newman, "unless you are going to the game. Gerald has already walked down with Phillip."

"I don't like football, Mrs. Newman."

"I'll bring up some molasses cookies in a bit. Go on up."

Tommy was propped up in a kind of fort of pillows, his eyes closed. "Hey, Michael."

Michael didn't now what to do, but it was very quiet and pleasant in Tommy's room. Indeed, it was Pearl's old room— which Michael had never been in. He'd imagined all sorts of things going on in that room. Now it was sort of a boy's room. There was a poster of Beethoven above the bed, and a music stand with some sheet music on it. Tommy also had a few clay figures that looked handmade lined up on his dresser. His schoolbooks were on a chair next to the bed. Plus other books.

"How are you doing?"

"Well, I can't see right now," said Tommy, his eyes still closed. Michael was able to really look at Tommy. His features were all like afterthoughts, just the barest curl of hair at the top of his head, his eyes dots beneath the thin-slash eyebrows, his mouth a small line. He was put together like a quick sketch. Somebody was bound to dub him Charlie Brown soon.

"Do you want the radio on?" Michael asked. Tommy had a cool old radio, but the boy said no.

"But you know what? Have you read Mrs. Momot's assignment?"

Michael had not, and there was a quiz on Monday.

So Michael read to him the opening pages of *Ethan Frome*, by Edith Wharton.

> *I had the story, bit by bit, from various people, and, as generally happens in such cases, each time it was a different story.*
>
> *If you know Starkfield, Massachusetts* ["that'll be on the quiz—Starkfield," said Tommy], *you know the post-office. If you know the post-office you must have seen Ethan Frome drive up to it, drop the reins on his hollow-backed bay and drag himself across the brick pavement to the white colonnade: and you must have asked who he was.*
>
> *It was there that, several years ago, I saw him for the first time; and the sight pulled me up sharp. Even then he was the most striking figure in Starkfield, though he was but the ruin of a man. It was not so much his great height that marked him, for the*

*"natives" were easily singled out by their lank longi-
tude from the stockier foreign breed: it was the careless
powerful look he had, in spite of a lameness checking
each step like the jerk of a chain. There was something
bleak and unapproachable in his face, and he was so
stiffened and grizzled that I took him for an old man
and was surprised to hear that he was not more than
fifty-two* ["That'll be on it, too—fifty-two."] *I had
this from Harmon Gow, who had driven the stage
from Bettsbridge to Starkfield in pre-trolley days and
knew the chronicle of all the families on his line.*

*"He's looked that way ever since he had his smash-
up; and that's twenty-four years ago* ["and that."]
*come next February," Harmon threw out between
reminiscent pauses.*

· · ·

*Every one in Starkfield knew him and gave him a
greeting tempered to his own grave mien* (What's a
mien? Tommy: means how a person looks.)*; but his
taciturnity was respected and it was only on rare occa-
sions that one of the older men of the place detained
him for a word. When this happened he would listen
quietly, his blue eyes on the speaker's face, and answer
in so low a tone that his words never reached me; then
he would climb stiffly into his buggy, gather up the
reins in his left hand and drive slowly away in the
direction of his farm.*

*"It was a pretty bad smash-up?" I questioned Har-
mon, looking after Frome's retreating figure, and
thinking how gallantly his lean brown head, with its
shock of light hair, must have sat on his strong shoulders before they were bent out of shape.*

*"Wust kind," my informant assented. "More'n
enough to kill most men. But the Fromes are tough.
Ethan'll likely touch a hundred."*

*"Good God!" I exclaimed. At the moment Ethan
Frome, after climbing to his seat, had leaned over to
assure himself of the security of a wooden box—also
with a druggist's label on it—which he had placed in
the back of the buggy, and I saw his face as it probably looked when he thought himself alone. "That
man touch a hundred? He looks as if he was dead
and in hell now!"*

*Harmon drew a slab of tobacco from his pocket,
cut off a wedge and pressed it into the leather pouch
of his cheek. "Guess he's been in Starkfield too many
winters. Most of the smart ones get away."*

"Can't blame 'em," said Tommy. And they both laughed for
a bit. And then it wasn't so funny.

Mrs. Newman brought up the cookies and seemed to have
been crying, even though she was smiling her bright smile.
It's just that Michael noticed her lashes looked dark, wet.

TOMMY NEVER DID GO BACK TO SCHOOL. Mrs. Newman told
Michael's mother that, first, a fever, and then problems with
his eyesight and headaches made it so he'd have to stay at
home. Michael volunteered to collect his assignments, with
Phillip in charge of turning in the homework. Although Tommy's time in the school was long enough to mark Michael as
a friend of "potato head," it no longer mattered. Everyone in
school forgot about Tommy Newman, like he'd never existed.
But to Michael, he existed, his only friend.

School was a joke, at least socially. Michael treated it is a joke, a bad, lousy, unfunny joke, and he kept to himself. He even brought out the Norton & Sons wardrobe on occasion, half to please his mother and half to rankle a couple of snickering guys and their attendant girlfriends. Wearing his shirt with a ruffle and narrow-legged pants with the stripe, he got the usual inarticulate comments. "Sit on this and rotate," he said to Dickie Trudeau, responding in kind and flipping him the bird. Dickie just looked at him like he'd seen something for the first time. He was amused.

Michael's father was just confused. Michael no longer listened to ball games with him on the radio in the kitchen. The World Series came and went in four dull games in early fall, after which Michael decided, by Thanksgiving or so, that organized football was a travesty. Michael still enjoyed throwing the football around with Phillip, teaching him to throw a spiral. But otherwise, he read his assignments, by himself in his room, and then, often, with Tommy in his room, and found that schoolwork was getting both easier and more interesting.

The Newmans treated Michael as more special than even the Dashnaws had. Mr. Newman showed Michael his collection of books: dozens of red leather volumes of Dickens, a whole shelf of green leather-bound Sigmund Freud. In the living room, he read *Life* magazine and *The New Yorker,* which had funny, confounding cartoons.

Although Michael's mother took note—and approved—of Michael's increased studiousness, his father took note—and no doubt disapproved—of his withdrawal from the great outdoors and the world of sport.

The only thing Michael did not withdraw from, with respect to his father, were their trips to feed the cows. He enjoyed rattling around in the smelly truck; he found his father increasingly amusing—or ridiculous—and treasured the chance to polish his disdain.

"Football's stupid, Dad. No individuals, just armies."

"An army won the war, wise guy."

"Baseball's boring. Nine guys standing around in a lot."

"Willie Mays doesn't just stand around in a lot."

Maybe this is what men do, Michael thought, toss strong opinions back and forth like a medicine ball.

"I don't trust shrinks," his father said.

I'm not surprised, said Michael to himself, sensing a power in silence.

Michael liked the barn's dark interior and the ripe smell of damp oats and manure and the comforting sounds of the cows mooing and clanging around, and even his father's animal sounds, the heps and whoas mixed with almost tender ministrations to his "girls." The girls were dumb and innocent and didn't really want or need much. And yet the little one, the mooley, distressed Michael. Each time his father had to wrestle the other cows, getting bigger and heavier now by the week, away from the salt lick or away from the slop barrel, Michael felt a wave of sympathy for the poor mooley.

"Why don't you get rid of her? Or give her back to someone."

"Not possible, amigo," said his father, who had started to roll out certain terms of masculine fellowship, like "pardner" and "boss," whenever they were at the barn. "You want her?"

Michael didn't answer, and there was nothing to say.

Since he'd turned inward (which is how he saw it, the image of a lighthouse beam reversed), Michael had more to think about these days. There was more light. He and Tommy talked about taxonomies and evolution. They finished *Ethan Frome* and then *1984*. Thanks to this, Michael felt he had a quieter and enlarged space, with more things to look at. He felt, somehow, furnished, lit within. All this owed something to the conversations with Mr. Newman, who welcomed the young boy's questions, particularly about math problems and the reach of the universe, and he answered them patiently. "You can't add anything to infinity, Michael, and you can't subtract anything from it. It has no quantity. It is nothing," said Mr. Newman, grinning. But it seems like everything, Michael thought.

II

IT WAS THE DAY AFTER THANKSGIVING and my father said there was something special going on at the barn and that I needed to come: He needed a hand. He said he might need two or three hands for this, and that he'd talked to Mrs. Newman about bringing Tommy along. Tommy had been feeling better since he'd gotten back from Burlington, where they'd drained some of the spinal fluid out of his skull. I remember thinking his head looked a little smaller and not as yellow. But he wasn't expecting to resume attending school.

I couldn't figure out what was ahead at the barn—maybe this was to be the day that the cows got sold. Maybe some dairy farmer would be there—or several farmers—and my father would have his big payday. I could see him wanting to share this kind of thing, with me and even Tommy. Show us the ways of the world. Farming, commerce, what men do.

It was a warm and sunny day for November. I remember I was wearing the sunglasses my mother'd gotten me for my birthday—aviators, for skiing, she'd said, though we were skiers only in her mind. When my father and I got to the truck, Ted Farrell was already sitting in the passenger seat. "Ted's gonna help us," said my father. He told me to hop in the back. Ted's collie Queenie was already there.

We headed up the hill and pulled into the Newmans'. I thought I'd have to go in and invite Tommy—ask him if he wanted to do this—but he was already on the porch with his mother, who was wearing her apron. He had a red hunting jacket on and the shades he had to wear lately to keep out the bright light. Ted got out of the cab and got in the back, insisting, as did my father, who more or less ordered it, that Tommy sit up front, which he did.

Ted said nothing to me as we headed up the hill to the barns. The wind was whipping his hair and ruffling Queenie's fur. You couldn't hear anything back there. They both had their snouts in the wind. I hunched in the lee behind the cab, trying to listen to what my father might be saying to Tommy, but I couldn't. When we arrived, my father went in the barn, emerged with a couple of items in his hands, and made a little speech, and Tommy and I stood together listening.

"It's the mooley's lucky day," he said. "Finally. As Mickey can tell you." My father looked at Tommy now, who glanced sideways at me, like, Why is your father talking to me?

"The little one in there we call 'the mooley' she's been getting pushed around for six, eight months. You know why? Because she has no horns. Born hornless. That's what a mooley is. A freak. One of God's mistakes. For a cow, hornless means defenseless. Same for any ruminant. But today, boys and girls, the mooley gets even. The mooley has her day."

He held up, in one red, filthy hand, a large pair of rusty clippers, and in the other what looked like a steam iron with a long cord that dangled like a live snake. He handed that to Ted Farrell. Then he waved us into the barn. It was dark as a dungeon. I remember Tommy and I both dropped our sunglasses on the floor and had to feel around with our toes to find them. And it was hard for Tommy to do such a thing—bend way down. I gave him his.

The mooley was released from her stanchion, and this is where Tommy and I came in: We were to watch her in the corner and hold her by a rope collar. Then Ted Farrell got on a barrel and with a long extension cord plugged his ironlike tool—it had a handle and a flat square surface of steel—into a socket. My father went around the front of the stanchions and, one by one, clipped the horns of a dozen cattle with a shocking crack, like musketry going off. Each cow nearly buckled with the pain and then set off to bucking. Blood that looked purple in that light gouted from the stumps and spread across their white-and-black faces. Ted Farrell followed, putting one arm around each cow's neck to steady her and apply the hissing iron to each stump of horn. "Cauterizing!" shouted my father at us over the din, by way of instruction. "Stops the bleeding!" More angry squealing. "Stops infections!" The mooley was jumpy in our grasp and confused and she looked at everything but what was right in front of her. She looked at me and at Tommy as if to say, Who's next?

"That's all there is to see," announced my father, though Ted's iron was still sizzling. He told us to take the mooley out, along with Queenie, and walk her around the pen.

The whole thing took all of two minutes.

When we got out into the barnyard, the day looked drained, like it, too, had been bled. I felt cold. I guess I was the one who was drained. But Tommy didn't look any better. His head was alarmingly white. It almost made me faint to look at it. At him. The low sunlight took some adjusting to after the dark interior of the barn. Queenie circled us as we stumbled some holding the mooley, who stepped carefully and kept shaking her head—quick little shakes. When I looked at Tommy, he had his eyebrows raised, which meant he was thinking, and was about to speak.

And I so wanted him to speak, because I was speechless. He rubbed his face hard and kept rubbing his face hard with one hand and he just never said anything.

We let the mooley pull us, guide us. We held on. It was a slow, sad parade, a staggering band with a cow and a dog. We sloshed through mud and cow shit till the mooley got to a destination—one of the salt licks. Her pink tongue stippled with black dots worked along the length of the white block, and it sounded like sandpaper. Then she seemed to sigh.

Tommy and I stood there, on opposite sides of the mooley, looking at each other. I don't think that we ever had another word. We drove back in the truck in silence, dropped Tommy off, and went home. The Newman family left Oreville in a matter of weeks.

III

"WHAT'S THIS? IS THIS IT?" It was Everett coming in from the stoop with the *Times* and the mail.

"Have you canceled the *Times* delivery for the month?" asked Michael.

"Have *you* talked to Ruben about picking up our mail?" parried Everett, handing Michael a small package that appeared to be a reused Jiffy bag, though it was carefully wrapped and Scotch-taped.

"This must be the Ellington CDs," said Michael.

Everett and Michael were having a Duke Ellington period— and they were about to take a road trip. The Public Theater was closed for renovation, freeing Everett, and Michael had finished his paper for the Math Society—it was now out for peer review. It was July 1 and they were quite ready to get out of New York.

Everett still played a little piano. He'd just read *Lush Life* and was obsessed with Billy Strayhorn. Michael thought a good selection of the Ellington band was in order—that lovely sonorous orchestral coloring, and the drive—to keep them driving all the way to Maine. And here it was—3 CDs, the Blanton-Webster years.

Michael noticed that the return address on the paper packaging—this was a used CD boxed set, ordered through Amazon but fulfilled by some private citizen selling his collection—was "P. Newman, 17 Harrison St., New Haven." And inside, taped on the edge of the jewel case, a tag read "From the library of Gerald F. Newman." Minutes later, Everett found Michael at the kitchen table, the CDs half-unpacked in front of him, the thumb and fourth finger of his left hand to his temples, staring at the opposite wall.

MICHAEL AND EVERETT DROVE UP 95 and listened to Ellington on the way. Michael was happy to have the new music—it relieved the need to talk. They found Harrison Street easily—they knew New Haven very well, having met at Yale in the late seventies when they were both in grad school. The big pale yellow house, three stories, however, they didn't know by sight—it was off Whalley Avenue, huddled in the shadow of West Rock. "A classic Queen Anne," said Everett as they got out of the car.

Phillip was getting a little portly and his hair was thinning, but Michael noted the same spunky grin that Phillip had when he was a kid, as if he was visibly savoring something he didn't need to share, but would, if you insisted. Michael had liked that in him. Michael, now sixty-five, figured Phillip to be about sixty-two. Phillip delivered a genuine hello and the men shook hands, all three around.

Phillip wore a pale yellow linen shirt with the sleeves rolled and twill trousers, while Michael and Everett, perhaps now a little embarrassed, were in sandals and cargo shorts. A woman stood on the porch, tall and trim in a floral skirt and white-collared blouse, looking, thought Michael, a lot like Mrs. Newman had looked on the porch of the house in Oreville when she watched them playing in the yard eons ago. This woman was Phillip's wife, and he introduced her as Janet. Bright blue eyes, a close-cropped head of silver hair. They invited their visitors in, and they sat around a large oak table in a room decorated with Palladio prints. There were fresh-cut flowers on a mantel; rugs; ivory-colored fabric lamp shades, like the old days.

"Original trim," whispered Everett as they sat down, "and wainscoting." This irked Michael at first, but perhaps it was polite to look around. "I think I recognize that piano," Michael said. A black upright sat in the corner. "Do you play?"

"That's a classic Story & Clark," said Everett.

"Janet does," said Phillip. "And yes, that piano's been in the family for years. We moved it to Oreville. And out of Oreville."

"*Used* to play," said Janet, correcting her husband. She'd left momentarily and was now returning with a plate of cookies.

"Molasses," said Phillip. Janet laughed self-consciously. Michael and Everett hadn't eaten since an early breakfast in the Village. There was already a silver coffeepot in the middle of the table, along with cups and saucers.

"Phillip told me that his mother always gave you molasses cookies when you used to visit their house."

"That's so true," said Michael, looking at Phillip, touched to have been remembered in that way—as a boy eating cookies.

"Mom also talked about it years later," said Phillip. "She remembered those times, short as they were, in your town. She also said that Tom was happiest then. You were his friend, Michael. She used to say you were his last friend."

There was a silence. Everett poured coffee for all. With some difficulty, Janet removed the plastic wrap from over the cookies. She seemed to have a bit of arthritis in her thumb. A smell of nutmeg and ginger wafted forth warmly when she succeeded.

"Well, how have you been, Phillip? You go first," said Michael.

Sleek blades of light came through the tall windows, the color of jade. The burl on the oak table swirled like nebulae. Michael felt a kind of radiant warmth from it all, suddenly very comfortable at this table in New Haven on a summer afternoon. He even put sugar in his coffee.

But Phillip remained silent, as if he didn't think it was his turn to speak, even though invited.

"So where did you move to?" Michael asked after a time, prompting.

Phillip then explained that the family had moved to Providence, for the children's hospital there—Rhode Island Children's. Tom—he was now Tom in memory, it seemed—had deteriorated rapidly. "The hydrocephaly stopped his brain from developing. It was like a slow flood. He gradually lost his senses. Sight, smell, et cetera. He was just shy of sixteen. The last months were rough. For everyone."

The reality of it hit Michael, even though his father had assured him that Tommy Newman "would never see eighteen," and his mother had agreed.

"We never heard from you," Michael said. Everett shot him a glance, but Michael shot it back in their secret semaphore, meaning, "That was no reproach."

And it wasn't taken as one. "My mother was devastated," said Phillip, looking down at the table.

"And how are they? How is she ... Hilda? And your father ... Gerald." Everett and Michael had already surmised that Gerald—"From the library of"—was deceased, though they could find no obituary online.

"Mom lost a battle with stomach cancer," said Phillip, straightening up.

"No!" Michael said, as if in protest. Everett shifted a little, knowing that Michael's mother had suffered the same fate.

"When?" Everett asked. "*His* mother died of that two years ago."

'I'm sorry to hear that, Michael. Mom died ten years ago last month. A blessing."

"Our mothers might have been good friends, you know, had we stayed," Phillip continued. Michael was instantly ashamed that it was Phillip saying this, and not he. "It's too bad," Phillip went on. "But we had to . . ." He hesitated, as if reconsidering, then plowed on. "To help Tom. Dad really thought it was best."

"Now you look good," Phillip said to Michael, lightening the mood. "Hair!"

Michael rapped his knuckles on the tabletop, looked at Everett, and said, "We've been lucky. Our health is good."

"I miss the paisley shirts," said Phillip with a straight face that meant the opposite. A tease. Everett and Janet exchanged exaggerated looks.

"And how's your father. How's Mr. Touhey?"

"He's no longer with us," said Michael. Everett managed to suppress some derision.

Michael went on. "Dad ended up at Sloan-Kettering. Bladder cancer. Just before Mom."

A dog barked then, somewhere in the house.

"I'm sorry, Michael," said Phillip. "Speaking of fathers, Dad's upstairs. That's his mighty mastiff barking now, Barley."

"Can I see him?" Michael blurted out. He might have regretted it . . .

Phillip assured him that he could. "Once the nurse comes down. Barley's barking at her; she's new." The faces of both Phillip and his wife were awash with affection, for exactly what, Michael couldn't tell, but what did it matter? Affection for the new nurse, the old man, the dog, each other. No, it didn't matter. There was plenty to go round.

"But catch *us* up," said Janet, now seeming nervous. "Oh, and let me say—we have no kids. Perhaps that's clear. I studied abroad and worked abroad, all over the continent, for twenty years."

"Neither do we," said Everett with a kind of theatrical fatigue, as if life were tough enough. And then he laughed. Janet smiled, but thinly.

"Janet was a portfolio manager with Deutsche Bank and then Credit Suisse," interjected Phillip, taking over, as Janet seemed to lose power. "We settled in New Haven when I became part of the faculty. I still lecture one term a year. And I have a little practice, restoring some of the old New England housing stock—like this place. I have a small staff—two partners—up in Hamden."

"It's good, then?" Michael said, unusually offhand for him.

"It's gorgeous," said Everett. "I hope we get a tour." Everett checked himself; his neck twitched, a signal that he was backtracking. He made things slightly worse, though. "Oh, but first, about us!"

Everyone waited out the awkward moment and let the goodwill return to the surface in the lovely room.

Everett reached for his third cookie. Michael commenced their overview.

"I graduated from Oreville," he said.

"He *escaped* Oreville," amended Everett, unable to resist.

"I studied at Cornell and took a degree in mathematics. Everett here and I met right in this town. I was in the grad school, applying theoretical models to biological processes. That's still my field. Everett was doing an M.F.A. Everett's in theater, at the Public Theater. Director of communications. We spent the eighties in New Haven. I've been at NYU, in the city, now for about twenty years, doing research mostly. Everett's gig with the Public is great. We travel. No children, two cats. We married last year. What else is there? Is that our life?"

"And Everett?" asked Janet. She'd just returned from the kitchen, again, and seemed restless. "Where are you from?"

"Oh, nowhere," he said, laughing his nervous laugh. Everett didn't like to talk about his military upbringing. He preferred to talk about decor or other people's families.

PHILLIP LED MICHAEL UP THE STAIRS to visit with Mr. Newman. Everett moved onto the front porch with Janet. Going up the stairs, Michael was reminded of the stairs in the Dashnaw house, and how it was down those stairs that first Phillip had come and then Tommy, when he first met them. Now it was in reverse, another mystery to be found. At the top was the big mastiff, swinging a light drool and eager for company.

Barley led the party across the hall to a large, sunny room. There in the bed, a big four-poster, was Mr. Newman, wearing blue pajamas, his right sleeve pinned.

He smiled broadly, his teeth gone gray, the skin on his face tight and shiny, cleanly shaven.

"Can this be Michael?"

Michael shook Mr. Newman's left hand, his one hand, like he had years ago, a loose gnarl of bones now. He shook it delicately, but Gerald Newman returned his grip with a sharp, strong squeeze.

"I remember you. You were good to our Tom," said the old gentleman. He smiled and sniffed a little, and brought a floral handkerchief to his nose.

"Thank you, Mr. Newman."

"You can call me Gerry now. No formalities. And frankly, you're older than I ever dreamed I would be. And here I am now, eighty-four. Five," he said, correcting himself, and Phillip, who stood some distance away, giving space, laughed.

"What are numbers anyway," Michael said. "Take it from me, Mr. Newman. Gerry. I'm a mathematician."

"Take it from me," said Mr. Newman with a topping grin. "I'm a shrink, retired. So little can be quantified, you know, when all is said and done. Sit down," he said. "Let's visit."

Phillip set a chair for Michael next to the bed, on Gerald Newman's good side, his arm side, and he extended his hand to Michael once again and Michael grabbed it. Phillip took a chair near the wall, and Barley positioned himself so he could see everyone.

Two hours later, Mr. Newman was asleep, Barley and Phillip had long since left, and Michael felt unburdened, sitting in the darkened bedroom. Something had brought them together, Mr. Newman had told him. Something had worked its magic to orchestrate their meeting again—he said that something was, no, not Ellington, but Michael. He said that Michael had a question. But Michael just shook his head and tried a smile.

"It was unacceptable," Mr. Newman then said. And they talked.

What was unacceptable was the scene in the barn—the mooley. Mr. Newman said Michael's father had tricked Hilda into letting Tom go to the barns—to pet cows, she'd been told. Afterward, Tommy was dropped off at home. He looked stricken; he was feverish and agitated, said Mr. Newman. He and Mrs. Newman got it out of Tommy what had happened. Mr. Newman called Patrick Touhey on the phone and they agreed to meet on the road between their houses, like some kind of showdown. Michael's father declared that being around a sick and doomed child wasn't so great for his only son, who was growing away from him, "his only father," Mr. Newman told Michael, quoting.

Mr. Newman said he made the decision, right then, as he walked back to his house, that it was time to move the family.

Mr. Newman was right that Michael had a question—but he didn't know it till he had the answer. The reason Michael never asked it was that Everett had always asked it for him. What did Michael's father do? What damage? What good? What was Michael, what was the father?

Michael then spoke—at Mr. Newman's request—about his math and biology work, his use of a model to investigate some of the data on the genetic diversity of small creatures, like plankton. "To our surprise, the idea of 'species' may not really be applicable in all cases," Michael told him. This was the subject of the paper he'd just finished for the Math Society. "Even among some very large populations, it's the individuals that matter."

"Plankton," Mr. Newman said softly before drifting off.

When Michael arrived at the foot of the stairs, he could see Phillip napping on the couch, a small tent of newsprint on his chest. He could hear laughter—Everett's—out on the porch, where he found Everett and Janet sprawled in Adirondack chairs, cocktails in hand. At Everett's feet the yellow Lab was recommending himself for something, anything. Janet looked up. "Everett's telling me about Fort Bragg," she said cheerily.

"Janet's an army brat, too," said Everett. He checked Michael's face for mood. "And we're going to play some piano four hands. Then order a couple of pizza's from Sally's—we remember Sally's—"

"Dad loves the white pizza," said Janet.

"—and then we're spending the night. And that's that."

From the shade of the porch, the sunlit lawn glowed like a host, its steady pulse a comfort, life itself, evenly trimmed. Images running the gamut of senses flipped through Michael's mind like cards in a trickster's hands—hay smell, summer light, his mother's chalky cheek, an empty shirtsleeve crisply folded, Ben Webster's breathy tenor, what love was, is, around him in repose on this porch. Molasses. This thought came to him: In an infinite field, the center is anywhere.

Sons

I

H<small>E SHOULD</small> G<small>OOGLE IT</small>—*roses of the unborn*—the random phrase flashes through. Meanwhile, he'll just mince around his midden of sneakers and loafers and those leather ankle boots she bought him that he hates and take another sip—the glass sits in a little sock cubby. It's dark in here. The liquid burns like distilled fire, which, in a sense, it is. Slow sips, coal smoke, Macallan in a California closet. Yessir. Not shit at all. Where was he? Joyce, perhaps. A little too romantic. Auden, maybe . . . Loved roses. The unborn . . . If he had his BlackBerry he could check it right now. He thinks he hears something. The She. He knew it. Good thing he's in the closet. And the She's out there—her shadow through the louvred door. Quiet now. He laughs—damn! But fuck it, it *is* funny. I'm a closet drinker is the thought he has just had, and it is funny, funny when the figurative becomes literal; that's comedy, isn't it? Make a note of it. The door opens and his heart does a gallop. Her face and hair and gray suit right there.

"I thought I heard something," she says. "Imagine my surprise." He can smell the acid of gone love in her breath, like ashes.

"I got lost," he says to wife number three, who just stands there, adjusting an earring with both hands as if tightening a bolt in a mask.

Several beats. "And now you're found again," she says in a mock-childlike voice, pivoting. "We'll be late for the theater."

It's Kerouac, he remembers, and throws back the rest of his scotch. "The roses of the unborn in my closed eyelids." *Big Sur.*

BORKMAN, BORKMAN, BORKMAN and the shit does not hit the fan. That's the problem with wife number three: She's got her own problems that she prefers a blind eye to be cast upon, her Tiresias, and he doesn't mind, and so she does not call her man on his scotch-in-the-closet trick. The quid, the pro, the quo. A classic codependency. She smokes and fasts and has her injections of Juvederm and Perlane; he has his five or six drinks a day, the patch, and an online gambling account. She has the indoor gym; he has the little writing studio. Little is done of late in either. But why mention it.

John Gabriel Borkman. Ibsen's next-to-last play. It's from the Abbey Theatre, Frank McGuinness directing. They are schlepping to Brooklyn to see it and they are late. Or at least they hustle down Church Street for the subway as if they are late. She welcomes the exercise, and he inwardly brightens at the prospect of an early arrival and time for a cold one in the lobby. It'll work out just like that.

Must we narrate the No. 2 train to Atlantic Avenue? It can be cut, in life's edit, if nothing happens or too much else of greater interest happens elsewhere. But give it a chance: they crush through the turnstile one after the other and actually touch, a bit of comedy, Keystone Kop–style, when he hastily steps into the same leg gap as the She and they jam to a halt, his front touching her backside, till he extricates himself with a backward hop. She actually smiles.

"Jesus, keen for Ibsen?" Lost.

The train is crowded—it is about 7:20, a Friday night. He checks his messages. She finds a seat, though, down the car, while he hangs on to his spot near the door. He can watch her. But not for long, for she is no one, looking at nothing, somehow. If there were a fire before her, she would not see it. She's moved to another world. She is looking at a child eating an ice-cream cone, one knee skinned and her Mary Janes dangling from a wicker seat while her father in suit and vest fans himself with a straw hat and checks his watch. It's 1960 and her eyes are closed. Her husband looks at the ad for Dr. Zizmor, dermatologist.

No message from the Guggenheim.

THE WALK FROM THE ATLANTIC AVENUE subway exit to the Academy is always depressing. On Broadway, or Broadway so-called, the theater you arrive at seems destined, as if, all along, that is where you were destined to be, like good drama—the Schubert! BAM still feels found by accident, an unfortunate one, and every time he goes there—or the She goes there (this was her notion)—you consider bagging the show, but there's no place else to go—no bars, no restaurants, just a few too many African import shops—and here you are. Up the steps, then, c'mon.

Pina Bausch that way. And *Richard III*. Beckett.

The place is charred and abraded and gray; warehouse chic, like most of hip Brooklyn today. But the concessions area is well manned and lively. The She repairs to the ladies'; he considers his fate through the rising vapors of a Sam

Adams, said fate, he concludes for the millionth time, long ago sealed.

After a human cattle walk up a side stairway, there is the stage, below. As promised (Ben Brantley), it's a snowscape. Ibsen, after all. Norwegian. The lights are still up; they settle into their seats, which are fair—but at seventy dollars each? What price culture, he thinks. For the moment, it is a New York moment—his fellow citizens, most of them white, like him, most of them in their fifties, like him, have worked their lives by some commodius vicus of recirculation, he thinks, to arrive here. So what. He gives the She the inside seat, more toward the center: always the gentleman. He must suppress a belch, while the She clicks to her minimal grateful look—a slight, momentary pinch of the outer rim of the nostrils, the mere suggestion of what sincerely tearful thanks would do to a face. Just a taste. Thank you. When she turns back to inspect the empty stage, he sees the dusting of powder on the down of her near cheek. Life is sad, Dad.

He stands to take off his overcoat—he loves this coat, John Varvatos, cashmere, a gift to himself for having finished his grant proposal on time—and now he will, yes, attend his electronics, as prompted by an announcement from the stage. He surveys the house. Ho: Below he sees his current in-laws, near the front, nice seats—why didn't he know the great ones were attending? They are old now. No reason, really, to hear from them. So he had not.

He could see the old man—the She's father—sinking into his own fine coat, hiding from the eyes of the public, hiding in plain sight, as it were, but drawing all the more attention to himself for disdaining it—just as he did when he read in public, quietly, rapidly, as if embarrassed to be the center of attention, but rather making the audience strain all the more to hear each brilliant sentence which, son-in-law must admit, each was. A genius fellow, agreed, who might be able to say more about Ibsen—who would be able to say more that is new about Ibsen, you can be sure—than anyone else alive, if he set his mind to it. Being in attendance, it is sure that he has put his mind to it. There'll be an essay in *The New Yorker* soon, no doubt. And a check, a certain slender portion of which, by virtue of the application of general principles and a provision of the tax code, will fall to his own account, or his wife's, Deo volente.

He'd seen the ghost of his own dear father once, in a public place, and wrote one of his better poems about it—at Shea Stadium, in attendance there with his own son (first marriage) at the time, and his son's girlfriend (she who had rescued him from drink—temporarily). His son was waiting out a court process in another state—wheels of justice grinding in Indiana. The boy with a substance problem; an anger problem; a problem with his own dad's abandonment of him when he was child, and yet sitting there together, the three of them, watching Mets-Phillies. Not bad. Not drinking, either, in support of said son. And then, there, before him, the baldish pate of his own late father, the boy's grandfather, dead by then for a good four or five years, a career corrections officer, and an Elk, a Knight, a Legionnaire. Dead ringer for the man, from behind: same soft hunch of the shoulders, too broad for the light cotton jacket that stretched across them; the slight tilt forward of the forehead, as if looking over glasses; the three strands of hair combed from right to left across the top, which his only son, as a toddler, used to pretend to barber with his fingers, sitting atop those shoulders; the rim and wattle of those ears unmistakable. He sits two rows down from them. The son—we better introduce by name here—Liam with his own son, Johnny, and girlfriend Leah; Liam's father, Frank (adoptive, ghost of?)—lies in wait, as the game progresses (against Curt Schilling, little progress by the hometowners), for the old man to stand up. He seems rooted to the seat; Dad had a different bladder than that, thinks Liam to himself. Surely, when the game ends or when the man with the baldish pate and the big ears decides to leave or take a leak, Liam will catch a glimpse. Frank, the ghost of Frank, will rise and turn and come up the steps, right by them. But he does not. The hometowners miraculously rally, knock out Schilling, and in the end pull the game out; Carlos Baerga, big night. The game ends on a home run—pandemonium, as they say. When Liam looks, the man is gone. A ghost. "Love is a distant whisper/and a listening in," he wrote in his poem.

The curtain—or rather, a scrim—rises. There's Fiona Shaw.

He'd seen her twice before—once at a party at the Irish consulate and then as Winnie in *Happy Days*, right here at BAM in a Deborah Warner production. At the party, a good ten years ago, Fiona was bright and vivid in look and talk, apple-cheeked, if not a bit windburned, her speech quite fast and a total delight, a sharp sweetness like, say, mint chocolate, her brogue. She sipped a whiskey, neat, and beamed at various men as if they were fascinating. In the Beckett play, she was too young for Winnie, Liam thought, her arms too gym-taut for a woman buried to her waist in a mound of dirt; and again tonight, she is too young for Gunhild Borkman, the shrewish wife of the disgraced John Gabriel. Sadly for Liam, Fiona Shaw is too young for him, as well.

She gives vivid speech once again as the play begins. Standing erect at center stage in blocky nineteenth-century shoes, she knifes the air with powerful strokes, cuts and shreds the space around her: Gunhild Borkman, disgraced wife of a disgraced banker, cannot be budged or fucked with; she'll gut you with flashing hands. She is emphatic and shrill. Her husband has cast the entire family into eternal shame by screwing investors, it would seem, and she's living with it, and he's living with it, in his eighth year of house arrest, or something like that, upstairs. Alan Rickman, as Borkman, once he arrives, drips scorn on everything with slow delight, ladling out bile. It's as if he's lost everything, including the chance to die. Everyone in the audience must be reminded of Bernie Madoff, thinks Liam. But Liam is reminded of himself.

THE NIGHT AIR SMELLS. Intermission. Liam stands outdoors on the top of the steps, where he'd be having a smoke if he still smoked. He is surprised that Borkman had gotten to him. He's never liked Rickman since his snotty embodiment of Eamon De Valera once. Unfair, yeah. But this one burned. Lost in thought, Liam is thinking about how lost in thought he is, which centers him a bit, and catches him up with time. He won't even sneak a drink in. A couple of typical BAM-ers ever so politely jostle him out of his way, assuming he is smoking out there in his big overcoat, but, rather, he is just then hunched slightly, trying to work the keys on his Black-Berry. A Google search:

> BORKMAN is of middle height, a well-knit, powerfully built man, well on in the sixties. His appearance is distinguished, his profile finely cut, his eyes piercing, his hair and beard curly and gray-ish white. He is dressed in a slightly old-fashioned black coat, and wears a white necktie.

Liam looks down at his shoes. The mica or schist or whatever it is twinkles like starlight in the cement—distant worlds beneath his Mephisto loafers. He has forgotten which tie he is wearing—flips it out and peers: the pearl grey Bax Agley. Almost like Borkman's. But he's not, what is it—"well-knit and powerfully built," but he's got a decent profile. He thinks. He shakes this thinking off—and Googles Fiona Shaw. . . . For crissakes, she's a lesbian, and they are flashing the lobby lights and he's got those stairs to climb and then the wedging in of bony ass to the unforgiving seat next to his wife of five years. As he makes his way slowly up the long cattle ramp, many of his fellow bovines slower moving than he, he gets in a few last glimpses at said BlackBerry: his e-mail. The Guggenheim, any day now, any day now. C'mon. Make me a Fellow or shoot me already. He has alerts set up—anyone who blogs with the words *Guggenheim Fellow 2011* will be a signal—to let him know who's won. No such alert. But here's one, from the "Brogan" alert. Something about his son from his son. What am I in, thinks Liam Brogan, a Paul Auster novel? The second act is gonna feature me?

He has no idea.

II

You gotta wonder why he showed me this, right? I mean, Taxi Driver. *I was six or so, I can still remember it. Just because he and Mom had seen it in England, who gives a shit—not a six-year-old seeing a bloodbath and a guy with a scary Mohawk, all in slo-mo. What the fuck. So it meant something to him. Maybe it reminded him of the disaster their marriage was? Of which I was the—whaddycallit?—issue. Fucking ironic. Here I am in a cheap motel, watching a cheap TV, watching Travis Bickle; watching Travis Bickle watch TV on TV, leaning back, tapping at the TV with his boot, like I could with mine, tap, tap, tap. Fucking boom it goes down. I could do the same but I can't afford it. I'll turn the sucker off.*

Johnny turns it off, from where he lies, on a bed, spread-legged, boots up, jeans, T-shirt, navy blue wool cap on with a big red *C* on the front ("Bears!"), in room 19 of the Motel Six outside Elyria. A Thursday.

He also told me fucked-up stories, like the one about Peanut. Stupid name for a dog, but it was a real dog in a real story and I came to love this story. But why? Peanut was a dog some farm family had back in the old hometown when he was kid. A big family—as opposed to Dad's, of course, poor little adopted boy and never had a dog, et fuckin' cetera—and a little boy in the big family sees Peanut, the family dog, a collie in my mind any-way, fuckin' around with a fox in a field as the kid is walking home from school or the milkin' or whatever, and tells his father, who thinks, "Rabies," and quarantines old Peanut by himself, because he's a cheap old farm fuck and rather than call a vet he figures to just keep an eye on the dog in the barn for two weeks and if no symptoms develop, then no rabies. The kids visit the poor thing, who was a proud farm dog, a hunter, every day and night, bringing him food and shit. And though he howls like a motherfucker at night, the kids hear him from their beds, star-ing at the ceiling, but Peanut looks healthy as hell, no problems, no problems develop, no hydrophobia, no foaming, and the old man decides it's high fuckin' time to let Peanut out, clean bill a health and everything, and they all go down to the barn to release Peanut before breakfast one Saturday and Peanut busts the fuck out of there past everyone and never looks back and they never see him again, off into the woods.

Dad—I'll call you Dad, okay Dad? [He says this, then turns to the little mirror over next to nothing]. *Dad said the story was about dignity; how Sir Peanut here felt wronged or could not understand what was happening to him, concluded, there-fore, in the manner of canine deductive logic that these humans were crazy or just couldn't be trusted by the dog world, and he just plunged out into the unknown, rather than run the risk of something truly nuts going on. Survival instinct. So Dad, just what is you telling me he-ah, to do the same fuckin' thing? To you? But I can't. I'm not a fuckin' dog, Dad. I am not, sir. Not a. Fucking. Dog.*

Johnny goes out into the parking lot and looks around. He looks around and thinks, Parking lot. I'm in an American parking lot, a way station, a place for my car. A place that waits for my car and a place my car leaves. It waits for every car, was built for it—any car can come. And leave. Every parking lot looks the same, standing on its flat pan—the faded black asphalt, the slowly erasing lines marking where to park, and not; the inevitable gravel, those small gray stones scattered like baby teeth. This lot is empty. He walked here, so it is partially his fault. But tonight—what night is it, what month?—Feb—the businessmen and, he thinks, out-of-town ball team are out to dinner or their game. They'll be back, in buses, in rented Hyundais. But right now, it is just him, Johnny Yeats Brogan, under an Ohio sky, and he's crying.

III

IT'S STARTING TO RAIN HARD IN BROOKLYN, hissing in sheets outside against the terra-cotta of the old Academy. The rain, and the trains rumbling underneath BAM, lend the third act a haunting musical score, as if things are about to collapse above and below. In the Ibsen play, set "in the neighborhood of Christiania," more weather—the wind howls outside the (one supposes) drawing room where the characters stand around and make speeches at one another. Borkman is in a strange spot for much of the act, literally—staked out near the wing. Marginalized. Liam has slowly become entranced by Rickman/Borkman. Rather, Rickman/Borkman/Brogan. That is, he identifies.

Borkman's got an embittered wife and a scheming ex-lover and these two women happen to be twins. The two women weirdly struggle over the fey son/nephew, young Erhart Borkman, a student, who is bland and unremarkable. No one gives a shit but the two women. Even Borkman's regard for his only son seems feigned. The lad's a fop—unlike Liam's Johnny, a tough, smart man who can handle himself, if a little too well; and his own wife, well-connected, coolly vain (hence distant: nice) and minding her own business—she has a difficult sister, true, but that's true of all three of his wives—endemic to sisterhood, it would seem. Still, when the self-possessed though ruined Borkman attempts to enlist his son in a new venture—what balls after his conviction for defrauding investors—a venture that will recover the family's pride and fortune, you have to admire the guy. Liam does anyway. Spunk. Defiance—acceptance of his guilt but, like, over it; others can be disabled by it— shamed; not him. That's what Liam needs—a little Norwegian backbone. A little courage; the word for it is *mot*. To stand there, as Borkman does, full-bellied, three-piece suit, accepting his guilt and yet radiating a defiant You can't kill me! Brogan takes this as a sign. He'll call Johnny tonight, or this weekend.

IV

ACT IV

BORKMAN.
[Not listening to her.] Can you see the smoke of the great steamships out on the fjord?

ELLA RENTHEIM [his sister-in-law].
No.

BORKMAN.
I can. They come and they go. They weave a network of fellowship all round the world. They shed light and warmth over the souls of men in many thousands of homes. That was what I dreamed of doing.

ELLA RENTHEIM.
[Softly.] And it remained a dream.

BORKMAN.
It remained a dream, yes. [Listening.] And hark, down by the river, dear! The factories are working! My factories! All those that I would have created! Listen! Do you hear them humming? The night shift is on—so they are working night and day. The wheels are whirling and the bands are flashing—round and round and round. Can't you hear, Ella?

ELLA RENTHEIM.
No.

BORKMAN.
I can hear it.

ELLA RENTHEIM.
[Anxiously.] I think you are mistaken, John.

BORKMAN.

[More and more fired up.] Oh, but all these—they are only like the outworks around the kingdom, I tell you!

ELLA RENTHEIM.

The kingdom, you say? What kingdom?

BORKMAN.

My kingdom, of course! The kingdom I was on the point of conquering when I—when I died.

ELLA RENTHEIM.

[Shaken, in a low voice.] Oh, John, John!

BORKMAN.

And now there it lies—defenceless, masterless—exposed to all the robbers and plunderers. Ella, do you see the mountain chains there—far away? They soar, they tower aloft, one behind the other! That is my vast, my infinite, inexhaustible kingdom!

ELLA RENTHEIM.

Oh, but there comes an icy blast from that kingdom, John!

BORKMAN.

That blast is the breath of life to me. That blast comes to me like a greeting from subject spirits. I seem to touch them, the prisoned millions; I can see the veins of metal stretch out their winding, branching, luring arms to me. I saw them before my eyes like living shapes, that night when I stood in the strong-room with the candle in my hand. You begged to be liberated, and I tried to free you. But my strength failed me; and the treasure sank back into the deep again. [With outstretched hands.] But I will whisper it to you here in the stillness of the night: I love you, as you lie there spellbound in the deeps and the darkness! I love you, unborn treasures, yearning for the light! I love you, with all your shining train of power and glory! I love you, love you, love you!

ELLA RENTHEIM.

[In suppressed but rising agitation.] Yes, your love is still down there, John. It has always been rooted there. But here, in the light of day, here there was a living, warm, human heart that throbbed and glowed for you. And this heart you crushed. Oh worse than that! Ten times worse! You sold it for—for—

BORKMAN.

[Trembles; a cold shudder seems to go through him.] For the kingdom—and the power—and the glory—you mean?

ELLA RENTHEIM.

Yes, that is what I mean. . . .

BORKMAN.

Ah—! [Feebly.] Now it let me go again.

ELLA RENTHEIM.

[Shaking him.] What was it, John?

BORKMAN.

[Sinking down against the back of the seat.] It was a hand of ice that clutched at my heart.

ELLA RENTHEIM.

[Tears off her cloak and throws it over him.] Lie still where you are! I will go and bring help for you.

[She goes a step or two towards the right; then she stops, returns, and carefully feels his pulse and touches his face.]

ELLA RENTHEIM.

[Softly and firmly.] No. It is best so, John Borkman. Best for you.

[She spreads the cloak closer around him, and sinks down in the snow in front of the bench. A short silence.]

When *John Gabriel Borkman* ends, John Gabriel Borkman is curled up, dead in the snow, and Liam is pale in his seat. Died of a cold heart, or a cold in the heart, did Borkman. An ice grip. In the final tableau, the shadows of two women—his wife and his true love, his wife's twin sister—stand over him. A weird triangle that Sophocles somehow overlooked; Freud, too. A genus of disorder that went extinct, thinks Liam, as he gathers himself up. He's glad to be out of there. Borkman showed him something, and he is anxious not to drop it, which he will, he fears, if he stops or talks, so he brusquely weaves through the crowd to the street and hopes (!) his wife will keep up, but she willfully tarries and dawdles and constructs a show tent around her own particular needs and it takes time to raise this tent and time to greet her parents and to say good-bye and strike the tent, so they will argue, he knows, when she is through and good and ready and gone.

V

JAMES JOYCE LEARNED NORWEGIAN in order to read Ibsen. It's tough to be in a bar in Brooklyn on a rainy night, after a row with your wife on the platform for the No. 2; after stomping off and out of the station, in protest and a certain coldness—from the She, from the surround, the ache-inducing iron and steel and the acrid tunnel breeze like death. That smell again. It's tough, but then, the night air is cold like a drink of water. You are thirsty for the water. And there's the soft orange glow of neon over there, some script in reverse on the damp street. Go there.

What was the fight about? The usual. He's too "distant." So there you are in a bar in Brooklyn on a rainy night; on a whim, you are reading letters written more than a century ago by two great artists. A scotch. There may be a hockey game from— Liam checks in for a minute—Montreal on the big screen, but Liam is in the archives of a defunct Irish newspaper.

> Jeg har ogso laest—eller stavet mig igennem en anmeldelse af Mr. James Joyce i "Fortnightly Review" som er meget velvillig og som jeg vel skulde have lyst til at takke forfatteren for dersom jeg blot var sproget maegtig.

Yes, Joyce learned Norwegian—Dano-Norwegian—in order to read Ibsen, and as an eighteen-year-old he wrote a review of what was to be Ibsen's last play, *When We Dead Awaken*—the play that followed *John Gabriel Borkman*. Ibsen got wind of it, somehow—he struggled to read the young man's review. He wrote a note in his own language, care of the *Fortnightly Review*, which Joyce translated:

> I have read or rather spelt out, a review by Mr. James Joyce in the *Fortnightly Review* which is very benevolent and for which I should greatly like to thank the author if only I had sufficient knowledge of the language.

And it's nice and warm in the bar. Liam Brogan is at one empty end, the glow of his BlackBerry dealing mysterious hands into his reading glasses, darting hearts and diamonds.

I wish to thank you for your kindness in writing to me,
wrote the young Joyce in reply, gamely in Norwegian. *I am a young Irishman, eighteen years old, and
the words of Ibsen I shall keep in my heart all my life.*

Another source Liam finds quotes Richard Ellmann saying,
"before receiving the note from Ibsen Joyce was an Irishman;
thereafter, he was a European."

> Your work on earth draws to a close and you are
> near the silence. It is growing dark for you. Many
> write of such things, but they do not know. You
> have only opened the way—though you have gone
> as far as you could upon it—to the end of "John
> Gabriel Borkman" and its spiritual truth—for your
> last play stands, I take it, apart. But I am sure that
> higher and holier enlightenment lies—onward.

VI

DAD,

I drank a fifth of vodka last night. A little unusual
as I usually drink half that to get me to that comfortable sleeping point. The night started off as a
celebration. I had tested out of a comprihensive
final exam. Although just a small insignificant community college class. I had done so well that the
proffesor decided that I had done enough to be
excused from the final two weeks and skip the final.
A proud moment for me to say the least. As I sat
at the computer trying to tell my tale to an assort-
ment of disinterested people, I began throwing back

the shots. Burning as it goes down. The simple act of holding the vile fluid in your mouth will induce vomit. I quickly chase it away with the soothing sweetness of cool green bubbly mountain dew. A flush of warmth grips my face. My mind begins to slip away from thoughts of bills and grdes and kids. I begin to aprediate myself. I start to feel great. To feel important and purposfull. I drink more taking it in easier and easier. To the point where the drink loses its toxicity, and takes on a life giving force. As if I am swimming in a different kind of water. Not the cooll awakening kind that most of us jump into. But a warm velvet like skin covering ever inch of my person. My movements become smooth and methodical. Making each gusture, each statement deep and meaningfull. I become insightfull, reflective. The next shot brings me to a point of thankfullness and regret about the things I should have done. The things I should have done. The things I should have done. The things I SHOULD HAVE DONE! A weight begins to pull on neck. My eyes noticeable become wet. Still high floating, near weightless I drink. My mother. Would she be proud? would she still love me? She Froze to death on a bender when I was ten. Fighting with one of her abusive boyfriends she tried to walk almost thirty miles drunk in a freezing rain. One more. She took her fucking clothes off! Why the fuck would she do that? In the snow and the ice she decided to get naked. The doctors said It was a natural reaction to hypothermia. Maybe she was just saying fuck it. Its cold I am drunk I cant stop drinking and whoever is in charg of this bullshit fuck you. The next one slides down my throat with no resistance. No need to chase it away. My body is ready. Receiving the poiso actively. My focus shifts to the consumption. I become clumsy now. Oops spilled my drink no. no. I caught it. Fuck! I spilled ths ash tray. I am smoking now. Nearly one for one with the drinks. I don't remember starting. I don't really want to but it goes on. Choking down the acrid smoke gulping down the burning clear fluid. Again. Again. Now two drinks in a row. I hate this fucking life. Fuck you. The house is a fucking mess dinner sucks. You are supposed to love me. Love me god damnit you fucking bitch you don't apreciate anything I do! fuck you! Get away from me! I hate you! All you want to do is take the kids away from me! The door slams as she storms out. What is her fucking problem? Another. I can feel my head slumped on my shoulder. My eyes are darting around. I am still sitting at the computer. I start to feel the urge to play sad songs. Songs that will make me feel. Songs that will make me cry. I want to cry. Secret tears. Tears no one knows about. Tears that are mine and mine alone. They need to come out this is their only release. A flood of emotions, a damn broken on a river of sorrow that builds for a lifetime. finally a chance to flow. I am crying now. Openly weeping. Why am I sad? why am I crying? why am I alone? One more. Its gone now. I smoke my last cigerette, wipe my face, and pass out.

Morning. Every one is mad at me. I am alone on the couch trying to dodge the resentfull glares of people. People who know me and love me. People passing by, trying to start their day. My mouth Feels filled with sand my head with cotton. I realize as I get up to piss. I had taken all my clothes off.

And somehow I'm here. In the Motel Six business center. Im gonna hit send. You won't believe how cold it is.

VII

"SOMEBODY SHOT OBAMA." The statement was heard, but apparently only by Liam. Then he heard it again. The bar was crowded now; it was midnight. All the young Brooklyn writers were there, as couples. They had nice clothes on, the women in flouncy dresses and fancy shoes, heels, straps across their long, bony insteps; the men in expensive sport coats over chambray shirts and flannel; they all wear stylish eyeglasses. Liam had been staring at them a long time. He places his hand across the forearm of a woman in a long dress and bandana who's been sitting next to him while he plunged through his BlackBerry. He's noticed her now. She seems like, well, a neighbor. She smells like that perfume that smells like pot and that Liam can never remember the name of. Howdy, neighbor. She turns to him, and she's the image of a woman on the cover of Brautigan's *Trout Fishing in America*. Arguably. Granny glasses. Gap-toothed. Loose. "Somebody shot Obama?" he asks her. "Really?" she says. "I'll tell my husband." Liam notes to himself: She said *rilly*.

She leaves a small stack of Kennedy half-dollars on the bar as a tip. The bartender—a narrow blade of a dude with an earring and a crew cut and a tight T-shirt—sweeps them away. "Mr. Clean," Liam surprises himself by saying. The bartender looks back and winks and shouts "Okay," over the din. "Quiet!"

Pointing a remote into the air in a *Sieg Heil* salute, the bartender turns one after another of the five TVs overhead from what was the traffic feed—Liam realizes the bar's called Traffic and the music just now being slowly turned down is "Low Spark of High Heeled Boys," the Steve Winwood piano running down toward silence—it's a high-concept bar, like out of a Jonathan Lethem novel. *He's* here, too, with wife #3. Why does Liam know this? It's like a dream, or some dreams, where you are character and narrator both. On television is the cock-jawed Brian Williams in a tux, looking grim. Everyone is watching.

IN THE BACKGROUND, in a bar that's emptied, a muted, off-key Chris Wood saxophone solo sounds. "Around this time, springtime, early April, on a Saturday morning there was nothing going on," says Liam. "Parents weren't around in those days to entertain you, take you to things. Dad had showed me how to fish; how to dig for worms and bait a hook and be careful. So some April days there'd be a smell in the air that made me want to fish; the smell sort of said, *Fish now.* And I would feel that it was good to fish; it was industrious; it was natural. The fish or the stream wanted me to fish." Liam dabs at a puddle on the bar. She stops him.

"The worms were there at the corner of my grandfather's garden, near the burn barrel, wanting me to dig them, bring them to some other wilder reality. And so I would go and get the round-pointed shovel out of the garage and bring the green bait can if I could find it or use one of the slender Prince Albert cans my grandfather'd discarded, a small tin flask with a snap top, and I'd head down the hill to the garden. I'd turn over six or eight shovelfuls of dirt thick as fudge and wait to see the purplish worm slowly squirming, sometimes only its tip visible, nosing around blindly in the fresh cut of air. I'd pry them out with my fingers and into the can they would go, with a little tuft of grass and the black dirt.

"The bait can would go in the creel; I'd check out the pole, see that it had a hook on it, Eagle no. 9; take a few extra hooks and a jackknife; there was a can of bug spray in the creel, old and rusty—Off.

"I'd walk up the hill past Ryan's Feed Store and up the old abandoned broken-up pavement along the brook. In the trees it was dark and the only sound was the rushing of the brook, always high in the spring with snowmelt. I'd get in deep enough and look for those pools Dad had told me held the promise of trout, as if they were lingering there, holding themselves steady and unseen beneath the surface, waiting for feed to wash through. Kneeling on the bank, I would begin the difficult process of baiting a hook, which began first with trying to extract a worm from the can; they all seemed to know how to burrow in and disappear; but one would soon be captured, and though it writhed in my hand, the barb of the hook sounded him into mindless pain and then surrender as his body, against its will and by degrees, became the meat sleeve of the barbed metal shaft.

"*Plink,* into the water the hook would go, the dark curl of meat tightening into a ball for a moment before unlacing and flailing there in the current. I'd wait in the loud watery din for a tug.

"When one came, it was like some stranger suddenly touching you intimately or somewhere where you did not control the reflex—a swab stick on your tonsil, the hammer tap below your patella. It got your attention right to your spine. The idea of a trout is pure muscle, the idea of twitch, muscle twitch defined against the press of the water, redefined at the end of the pole in your hand when the trout flips into the free, wary air, snapping back and forth like a wound up something, and you start marching in a controlled panic, your sneakers splashing to land the snapping catch into the brush, where you don't care if the reel gets wet behind you or if the line tangles as long as you get that trout, furiously snapping its green silvery red-speckled body, hung up on a branch.

"You have learned to handle it—to palm the sticky cold fuselage in one hand and with the other remove the hook as humanely as you can. The blood is thin, a smear of it. It smells fishy; the worm is there, limp as a soaked shoelace. With a slight crunch, the hook is extracted and the trout, its eye dull and disbelieving, is then dropped in the creel and the top shut fast. He whops around in there for a good half hour while you recompose yourself, untangling your line, and fantasizing how many more you will get, till you don't hear the trout moving anymore, only the roar of brook and some stones tumbling."

"Why'd you tell me that?" asks the woman in the granny glasses, who is back.

"Because somebody shot Obama," he says. "And I want to fuck you."

VIII

Dad,

I can remember the first time I was exposed to people in my family drinking. It was a fantastic time for me as I was just about six years old and all was good in the world.

My grandfather had a band. A Mexican folk band made up of local friends and associates. Plymouth Indiana had a large Mexican population on one side of town, My grandparents were one of the first families to settle and work in the town. Hard working and proud. My grandparents refused to completely assimilate to white middle American life. In fact they flaunted their own culture every chance they could. Singing and dancing in the old way. Eating and drinking the same types of meals their parents had eaten Years ago in Brownsville Texas just a stones throw away from Motmodos Mexico.

My grandfather was tall and lean with hands that could crack multiple walnuts in one effortless constriction. His skin reminded me of a baseball mitt freshly oiled. His broad grin was accented by two gold teeth that sparkled at you when he spoke.

The band itself had a bass, Guitar, drums, and at lead vocals and accordion my grandfather. Nearly every weekend The kitchen would be filled with wives prattling on making tortias, drinking sweet sweet coffee, and smoking cigarettes. While the basement was filled with the men. Drinking and smoking cussing as men do when woman are not around. Playing hours of beautiful music that wafted up the stairs reminding every one who heard it that they were Mexican and proud of it.

The drinking was a mandatory affair with the stingy smell of tequila and the mustier smell of beer being mixed with the heavier smells of damp concrete and mold. Between songs of tears and songs of joy. The shots were thrown back and the beers were gulped down. The women never drank. I can remember thinking that that was odd. But the boys down stairs got roaring. The separation of the men from the woman was a good way to hide how much was actually being consumed. The woman never went down stairs. If food or coffee were needed below, it was my job to ferry between the two parties. It was as if the men were slightly embarrassed. And the woman were turning a blind eye. I can remember the guys always pissing in a white bucket in the corner. Avoiding the stares of the woman all together.

I never remember a hint of trouble. My Grandfather could hold his liquor. So could most of his buddies. Hard working former field workers all, Cowboy boots that glistened and came to fierce points. Cowboy hats with feathers and buckles. These to me were some of the coolest dudes I had ever scene. My grandfather the coolest of them all. All six foot three of him, his huge ribbed accordion hanging from his shoulder. His right foot always tapping he would work the accordion back and fourth the inside looking blood red when open and gold leafed when closed. Long slender fingers contorted over bone colored buttons. His voice would go deep and sympathetic. His Spanish flowing out of him as if from another time. Nearly gone now.

It was in that basement watching the boys jostle and drink and laugh. Through that smoke filled haze I watched with wonder knowing that one day I would be a man and It would be my turn to drink and play even maybe I would get a chance to piss in that bucket.

IX

HE IS READING AN ALICE MCDERMOTT NOVEL on the No. 2 train. He could not find a cab from Miss Trout Fishing's Fort Greene apartment at 3:30 A.M. So he is reading the book, which he found in her lobby—a giveaway—on his way out. He always needs something to drink or read during travel; preferably both. Otherwise, travel is intolerable; it makes his skin needle with impatience to be touching something other than fabric or air.

Liam picks up at a part where a young man is on an airplane for the first time, rising high above Queens, headed to boot camp. Ironically, he's traveling, too. It is 1969 and the fellow's been drafted. From the window, he looks for his neighborhood below; he thinks of saying a prayer. He thinks of Jesus' thought the night before his Crucifixion: "Your will, not mine." The young fellow on the plane amends the prayer to "Give me a break." A fine prayer, thinks Liam, who slowly becomes aware that a guy on the subway is addressing him—a steady, droning voice that he has been tuning out is directed at him. What's the guy saying? "Are you related to Dr. Zhivago? Are you related to Dr. Zhivago? Are you related to Dr. Zhivago?" That's what he is saying. It's a homeless fellow, with no socks, bare shins with open sores. Unkempt hair, wild beard, glint in his eye. Liam is in his fine overcoat, with gray scarf, his reading glasses, his trimmed gray beard, looking, he imagines, gaunt and hungover—did he even eat dinner? Liam's just finished a chapter, so he closes the book.

"No," he says to the fellow. " I'm not Russian."

"You're not Russian," says the homeless guy, delighted to be spoken to. "You're Irish, then?"

"Yeah, I am actually."

"Well then," counsels this homeless chap, "say a prayer before you go to bed tonight. Say a prayer and then go to bed."

X

NOBODY SHOT OBAMA. Somebody shot *at* him. It is all over the TV when he gets back. The She is already in bed. The whole event or nonevent has probably passed her by. Beauty sleep required. It is 4:00 A.M. and he can still smell Miss Trout Fishing on him, sweat and, yes, patchouli. "A bushy herb of the mint family," she replied when he asked, "with erect stems." That did it.

He sits in his own study. Friday's *Times* sits there as well, unread. He'd sleep here tonight. He takes the CNN feed on his Mac. Over and over, barely legible to his blear eye the strip—"Breaking Story: President unhurt. Feds in pursuit of shooter." Above that, in a loop, the now-famous River-walk Barbecue in Kentucky. A stage, some bare trees; a casual Barack in a light jacket bouncing lightly to a podium; grade schoolers in uniforms around him and then a shot—a shot!—not like anything else, not like a firecracker; we've heard shots now; we know shots—a gunshot concusses, then everything is after, a stampede; a camera takes up a good load of shoes and scuffling and dirt before catching a wheel of empty sky and the tree limbs and some man's hat and collar before finding the stage in a crush of dark suits, then a wobbling close-up of several people leaping off stage left, getting away. The film then goes grainy and slows down as CNN focuses on the fleeing people. That's when Liam spots his tweed coat.

XI

LIAM HAD ALWAYS HAD A THING about coats—coats and jackets. For a guy not too materialistic—not willfully, anyway; he'd traveled light in life, leaving trunkloads and boxfuls and shelves full of possessions at many an abandoned outpost like a routed fugitive—he had love affairs with his outerwear, provisioned for transit. It's not that he accumulated a lot of coats and jackets; in fact, if he had, there would not be the kind of obsession with them that was his own. It was the very sparseness of his collection that impassioned him so. A new coat meant something; it was a commitment to a style or a spirit of acquisition that carried with it either much about who he was at the moment or who he intended to be once the thing showed up and he grew into it over a couple of winters, or autumns, or bracing springs. There was the heavy yellow leather jacket his mother had bought for him; she had encouraged him—she still a denizen of rural upstate, he the prodigal in Manhattan—to wear less black and more bright colors, "for your eyes!" she'd said, which she'd always called hazel but which everyone else thought were brown. Sure, Mom. She'd sat smoking in the car in the mall parking lot in Plattsburgh while he'd ventured into an empty Ralph Lauren and bought with her credit card a heavy leather car coat because he was connected to this place and this woman's (fading, sweet) vision of him, her only son. Why not.

He loved that coat.

After she was gone, there was the wool brown-and-black "upland field jacket," with deep button vest pockets for carrying shotgun shells, that Liam got from L. L. Bean. He wore this upstate as well, touring the place, his old haunts, the cemetery, the abandoned iron mine, with his son, little at the time, who was visiting. Those pockets, Liam found, as if surprised, were deep enough to conceal an eight-ounce flask for their father-and-son walks in the crisp sunshine, picking up sticks and stones and bouquets of late wine red sumac along the abandoned D&H tracks.

He loved that coat, too.

There was a reversible Italian jacket, cashmere blend on one side, faint wool check on the other; and a black cotton painter's jacket from Paris, whose plush nap he had striven to preserve by not bending his elbows much, till he forgot. After several drafts of "My Coats," which was the third or fourth part of a larger and eventually abandoned work featuring similarly descriptive and emotive lists of kitchens he had known, women he had slept with, ball games he had seen, and fountain pens he had had some relationship with, some therapist or another talked him out of this approach, not long after he got his fifth or six rejection from literary magazines. No one was buying this stuff.

One of the later jackets, however, was part of his roots phase (birth parents found—Donegal)—an Irish tweed. He'd always wished to have a handsome, warm, genuine Irish sport coat you could button up and wear in the brisk and rainiest weather, and he found one in an online catalog, from Cleo's in Kildare Street. He loved it, but it fit so poorly that people commented. So he put it away, after turning himself around in front of the long mirror in the men's room at the Old Town one afternoon. Yes, it flared out and made his ass look big; there were two vents, on left and right, which looked more like mud flaps. The left one, for some reason, through some accident of stitching, actually curled upward, as if it were a shingle about to peel off. Unsightly to have this over one's buttock. And anyway, the jacket was too broad in the shoulders, making him look smaller than he was—like the old Irishman he wasn't ready to be quite yet.

But it was a five-hundred-dollar item, and when son Johnny told him he was going to a Notre Dame football game with the son of the boss of the machine factory where he worked, Liam said, "I'll send you something to wear to the game."

And there was no mistaking that turned-up flap at the backside of the burly, dark-haired fellow vaulting off the stage at the Riverwalk Barbecue in Paducah, Kentucky, playing over and over on CNN.

LIAM KEPT WATCHING IT TILL MORNING, which came very late.

I should've done, I should've done, I should've done, Liam snarls to that image of himself in the mirror that just reverses all his flaws. He claws his own cheek and brings up three red trails. *I should've prayed for my son.* That was Jesus on the 2 train.

And I will; he nods to himself in the mirror, his face pain peaking righteously. At his feet, his packed bag. The sun just coming up, gilding the tops of buildings he can see out the bathroom window to the west, in Jersey City. I'll say a prayer tonight from a mountaintop. One last look. Light off.

XII

ON THE AVENUE, IN THE SUNLIGHT, even at this hour, a Saturday in February—with the Super Bowl tomorrow!—a significant mass of traffic passes in a slow, powerful roll. Buses lug forward; cars in their steel and sprung weight maneuver—so many cabs, and leaning bikers, quick as a painter's stroke on the gray pavement, zip between objects. Stolid pedestrians move so slowly, some locked in conflict on cell phones—that black woman—"Everything I gets is from me; if I move to Florida, it because of me; if I get a Benz, it from me; if I move apartments, it from me; if I make a life change, it from me, muthafucker. Not from you!"—and others, so many quintessential New York faces—great-nosed, small, dapper men with combed-back silver locks, striding as through water; a leggy gazelle with her Ford Agency portfolio canted awkwardly on a beautiful keel of a hip, teetering on heels; she's smoking a long cigarette; a little guy looking like his dad, who walks beside him, both in Steelers gear, jabbering, comically trying to match strides. A smooth biker, haughty like some aristocrat of street travel, flies by in some conversation with the street or himself; you somehow lock visually to his left ear, yellow through a helmet hole, and follow him for a block in that small world, his pumping, what he hears. You wonder where he's going, or what his mother thinks of him, and does he care.

Such interiority, once such a comfort, then such a danger, is, in its way, a comfort once again, though the means of achieving it, as an adult and not as a safe and daydreaming child, are toxic: We're talking about booze.

Liam has taken a potion on the way to his garage, where he keeps, unbeknownst to anyone, his Jeep—paid for in cash. The She never knew. The garage rent billed to his studio address, and fuck the insurance—he's careful, he needs to be discreet more than he needs to be protected—he pays for minimum coverage once a quarter, again in cash. If he hurts anyone, the aggrieved may get the place in Harrison. Life's a risk.

His potion isn't taken in much of a joint—not every place has the shutters up at 7 A.M., but Blue Ruin does, a place named after a Prohibition bathtub gin that'd kill you, and situated in the shadow of Port Authority and a block from his cheap garage. Tracy's there, the barkeep, and she's been there all night, by the looks of it. Liam can see thin lines of grit in the creases of her neck. Two double screwdrivers and a black coffee from the next-door deli—no smokes, of course—and Liam is ready to go to the mountaintop. On TV he watches every bit of every moment of the looping shot in Paducah seen round the world. And now some believe Obama really was hit. Where is he? Fox wonders. They have a reporter at Walter Reed.

Fuck the president, thinks Liam. Where's my boy?

Turns out, by midday, Fox will be wondering that, too.

THE SUN SPILLS YELLOW across the windshield—like chicken gravy, thinks Liam. He's navigating within the thickening Saturday-morning traffic, like a giblet—in chicken gravy, thinks Liam. The sun isn't yellow it's chicken—he's listening to Dylan, and Dylan for the moment covers everything—like . . . He won't do that. He turns the music off and switches to radio and reminds himself again that he still doesn't smoke. Oh, how cigarettes used to punctuate the road trips—life measured out not in coffee spoons but in Marlboro Lights—one per county he used to try to do—city, Westchester, Putnam, Dutchess, Columbia, and so on, but always doubled up on each, at least. Still, it was worth the effort. Living longer now, look out! He is over the Spuyten Duyvil bridge now and had better pass that belching panel truck. He gets winding along at better speed and on into rocky Riverdale, light glancing through the bare trees. He realizes he is still scanning through stations on FM mindlessly—without hearing, anyway—and begins to listen. NPR will have something—would it be all-day coverage? The welfare of our president, and the search for the would-be assassin, full team coverage. This should be good, thinks Liam as the back vent of his old tweed coat flaps at him like a signal of hello in his mind, and he wonders, How? What if? No. The road banks and torques under a stone bridge, and a block of Tudor homes crisscrosses in his vision. He can hear Scott Simon, still misses Daniel Schorr, and his heart is pounding and the car is stopped and steaming and there is a rocky outcrop with a bush and a Gristede's bag caught in it right in front of him. His face is hot and he hears something strange, like a little boy's voice asking, Are you okay, Dad? Are you okay? Or is it, Are you a hockey fan, then? Are you a hockey fan, then?

When he wakes up, it is with a sense of embarrassment—it is the embarrassment of drool on his chin that has roused him to consciousness and the sight of a young man's face framed with unruly hair—What are they called? Dread something. He can't think—looking right at him, his eyes speckled and bright with youth, and he is asking if he is okay.

I don't know, says Liam. Who are you?

You took a bad turn, says the kid. This ain't the road here. It's like a little service road, just from here to right over there. Some kind of turnaround. You okay?

No answer.

Your Jeep looks okay. The brush and stuff slowed you down. You almost killed me, though!

No answer.

Listen, sir, you okay? The cops'll be here quick, if you want that.

That gets Liam's attention, and he grips the steering wheel hard and winces in pain, like he'd been grabbed by something steel. Both wrists screaming, now held limp before him like dead animals.

You must've sprained 'em, said the kid.

No answer.

THERE'S A HOSPITAL UP HERE A BIT, says the kid, who is driving now.

No no no, says Liam. What?

You need a hospital, for your mitts. And a garage, for the Jeep, or both.

No answer.

What I need—should anyone ask!—the kid says it as a theatrical aside, half over his left shoulder, as if there was a passenger behind him, offstage as it were—and Liam realizes with a shiver that the kid is narrating himself.

Did you say, *as the kid says as a theatrical aside?* asks Liam.

Hey, he speaks, says the kid, says the young man.

Pull over, says Liam.

I won't. Can't. Not here. No room on the shoulder. That was your mistake, Pops.

Hey, the kid continues, looking at the old man, I called you pops, and you got a bump on your head.

IT'S A LITTLE HOSPITAL IN ELMSFORD, the parking lot, and Liam is standing beside the Jeep, bent over, vomiting. Like chicken gravy, he thinks to himself, and then says it aloud, straightening up, laughing.

I'm an asshole, he says, looking skyward, whispering it. The sky is far and gray, and he looks into it, blinking away the shards of tears on his eyelashes. He tries to travel mentally, projecting himself, such as he is, as an entity higher and higher into the upper atmosphere, seeing that little sad tableau below—a red Jeep poorly parked in a half-empty parking lot with two chaps standing either side of it, looking lost. Not even a father, not even a son.

He's feeling better.

THEY ARE HAVING A DECENT BREAKFAST at the El Dorado Diner in Elmsford. They are almost out of the city, almost across the Hudson. Almost gone, Liam is. And he really rallies, over a short stack and scrambled eggs. The kid has a chef's salad and a seltzer. Liam considers a Bloody Mary—he could use it—but decides for the moment, his breast flushing with pride, that he will not corrupt the youth—or his driver.

The kid says his name is Henry Gibson—at which point Liam orders a Bloody Mary.

Did you say, you did, Henry H-E-N-R-Y Gibson?

Yeah, Pops.

Not Henrik Ibsen. Hen-Ree Gib-Son?

Yeah. It's a simple name.

It is, it is. But it sounds like—do you know what a homophone is?

An instrument?

No, no. You're a sweet kid, Henry. No. I just saw a play last night by Hen-Rick IBB-sen. A great Norwegian playwright. Say it fast—say your name fast.

Interesting. The kid picks around at the curls of ham that sit atop his salad. Liam draws on his Bloody Mary. This is not that interesting, to the kid.

It gets worse.

Did you know—of course you wouldn't know—that when

I was your age there was a comic—he was from around Philadelphia—who took the name Henry Gibson in drama school
because it sounded like, it was, a spoof on Henrik Ibsen, the
playwright. *A Doll's House*, stuff like that. And the play I,
er, we, saw last night. By the unexciting name *John Gabriel
Borkman*.

The kid drums his right-hand fingers on the tabletop, but
silently.

No. I mean no, I didn't know that.

Spicy, Liam says, trying a weak whistle. The vodka brightens his eyes. His mood. His hands still hurt, but a little less.
His head still throbs, but a little less. He jumps up—somehow renewed—and grabs sections of the *New York Times*
spread out on the adjacent sit-down counter.

So, who do you like in the game tomorrow, kid?

The Super Bowl. I don't care much. I play music.

Liam is plowing into his pancakes, his palate absolutely
alive from the spicy tomato juice. He's never tasted pancakes
this good—and from the El Dorado Diner, no less. I like
Green Bay. I've got a hundred units on 'em. I gave the points,
he mumbles to himself, distracted.

What do you mean, you play music? Liam notices a stout
waitress lingering, with a look on her face that says she's spotted a pederast, or doesn't like the look of a slight black kid
having a meal with an older white gentleman. Crime's all
over—and in her precinct! He puts down the sports section.

I play, man, the kid says, and then hauls up a black trumpet case, holds it there for a second, and then returns it to a
spot under his chair.

Oh really?

I'm on my way to Montreal, to see Roy Hargrove. Do you
know Roy Hargrove?

Liam nods and smiles and leans back. He wants to just listen, as does, apparently, the waitress, who busies herself at a nearby table.

But the kid returns to his salad.

Well, then, what about Roy Hargrove? says Liam. No, I don't know *anything* about Roy Hargrove. Tell me.

He's my teacher is all. A great, great horn player. He's taught me a lot. And that's why I was hitchhiking on the Saw Mill. To get to Montreal. He's playing at the Monument National, Sunday night. Tomorrow. He's left a ticket for me.

LIAM IS CHARMED AND WARM and getting comfortable in the front passenger seat of his Jeep. He's asked to see Henry's driver's license, and Henry, producing a legitimate Delaware card, has agreed to chauffeur them north, as that's where they both are heading, though Liam has a destination short of Montreal. At least it will get Henry, they figure, four-fifths of the way there.

The kid's got quite a story, and a lot like Hargrove's. Hargrove played trumpet in the high school band in Waco, Texas, back in the eighties, when Wynton Marsalis visited the school. He spotted the young man, then sixteen, and got him a scholarship to Juilliard. It was Hargrove twenty years later, visiting a YMCA in Philly, who spotted Henry, and worked the same magic. Henry's family was poor, and living and studying in New York, even on scholarship, has been tough.

Henry is eighteen, according to his license, born on the Fourth of July. Like Satchmo, Liam thought.

Liam then told the kid everything he knew about jazz.

WHICH WASN'T MUCH. He only knew the stories. He didn't know anything about the music, all the stuff the kid knew. He knew Charlie Parker—Liam listened to Phil Schaap's *Bird Flight* for years, the entire chronology of the recorded Bird, but wouldn't know a chord change from a key change—though he knew that it was Bird's changes that made him a legend. But he went on.

Now kid . . .

I invented you as a plot device, says Liam as Henry turns cautiously back onto the Saw Mill River Parkway. Now I can drink and drive, and still keep myself on the right side of the law—most worthy of the sympathies I hope to attract. It's my genius, you see: I drink; *you* drive.

XIII

HE TRIED TO TELL HIS STORY in several voices. He could never find one. The first person was his first choice and the obvious one—this is my story. The *I* has the authority of firsthand experience of the tale to be told; incident and emotion are conjoined in the one, the first. There's no guessing at how love or pain affects the *I*; for I will tell you. And life's early stories are filled with emotion and a kind of amazement at emotion—a thrall—to feelings that are being felt for the first time; the early stories are filled with accounts of events experienced for the first time. It's the coming of age and its first voice is often first person.

That's not to say that one outgrows the first person and then it is of the past. And he did not believe that, as, on the contrary, the first person and the novelty of experience appealed as an option for the telling throughout his life. And every time, from first to last, he discovered that, perhaps for want of genius, perhaps not, his story was not his own; he did not possess himself or his tale. Because there were more people in his story that were not him. What could *I* tell about them? And who cared to know the limits of what *I* knew?

Third person suggested itself, and often did so first. A thousand times abandoning the first will eventually recommend you start somewhere else. A dog would do it. And so would he. Like now. The spirit of some intelligence, disembodied, grazing over incident and time and conveying what happened, happens, and is said or thought or felt. But third person, in the end, is always too scary. It is like a hand grenade in the pantry. It has too much power; it might go off. If it knows everything, then what doesn't it know? And wouldn't it always have to tell? If it doesn't know, why doesn't it know? What is it? How can the authority of a story being told reside in an unknown force? Who made it God? Is it a device or is it an ideology? Is there a person in third person? And what's he doing in my kitchen? The kitchen is mine.

Frustration leads to the final choice—the second person. This is death. This is the intimate accusatory voice—sharp and deadly whether accusing the self or others: "You are the body and the blood." Really, who says so? You?

The different voices, different tenses even, have their appropriate moments and applications. Liam's work—his career, for better or worse—consisted of a series of weakly related pieces, poems and stories and memoir essays, composed over a thirty-year period, each apt enough for the time and its modest ambitions. But as to a larger work—his capstone, as he would have it—*that* called for something more sustained in execution and broader and deeper in ambition, and he could not settle on a person, much less a place or a thing.

Then he seemed to have it, somewhere up the Taconic. Somewhere up the Taconic, rolling through the tight corners and rock-shaded glens, he'd begun to fade. He'd managed to establish a deal with the kid—one hundred dollars Liam gave him, right there, on the dashboard, yours, to drive him north; he'd established that the kid could drive and was decent company—though he was quiet, the kid had told a sweet, economical story about the trumpeter called Brownie, who was the sweetest man with a "buttery" tone and he didn't do drugs or drink and was a math whiz and was killed in a car wreck at night in Pennsylvania, and the kid, the kid said, would drive careful and slow. Is that okay? Because if it isn't, I can't take your money.

And by then, Liam is in a dreamland raked by the shadows of bare trees in a space and day emptied of color or perhaps drained of it as when you are about to pass out, all the familiar objects around you turning slowly and evenly white and then there is a filling up; the air around things fills with a pale tea. The car sounds rock him as a child is rocked in days of old in the back-seats of deep-seated sedans, the growl of the engine jiggling your diaphragm pleasantly and your world takes place in a black boxy shape of space in the foot well behind your mother's seat.

Liam saw what he should do, and it was a confusing thing, complex and simple—give everything all you have all at once. That is, it was the road that would save him (now that he had a driver!), the road swerving through familiar towns and stretches, allowing him to move nowhere while traveling, to think of his wife and what to do, his son and the trouble he's in, his own work, how to fashion it all as his own; this boy here; the blues, the blues as art form, and why not: a buttery tone.

XIV

LIAM ACTUALLY KNEW A LOT about Brownie, or Clifford Brown, the brilliant young trumpeter out of Wilmington, then Philly, whose inventive playing and spectacular technique—and that round, warm tone—caught the attention of Gillespie early, and then Max Roach, who formed a band partnership with then twenty-two-year-old Brown. He was the present and future of jazz till Bud Powell's brother's wife ran the car off the road at night in rural Pennsylvania, killing Brownie, Richie Powell, and herself, ending something, making Brownie part of jazz's past. It was a loss that shook a lot of players—like Scott LaFaro's death in a car wreck would clobber Bill Evans five years later. Liam had seen the play in New York that won a Tony and featured the main characters sitting around in the last scene listening to a Clifford Brown solo played at a jam session—a five-minute marvel of all that Brownie brought to the art of the horn. He'd always thought that, after the tape picks up Brownie thanking the crowd, and saying he has to go, it's such a hot night, and, well, good-bye, that he'd gone out and got killed that night; the kid corrected him.

That's what people say 'cause it seems true, but it's not. They want it to be true. Weird. When it's not. What it is is the last sound we have out of Clifford—it's hot, he says. And then you know we don't hear anything again. But it was a couple of weeks before the car wreck.

Liam made a mental note—Get the Clifford Brown biography—just as he drifted off toward sleep near Jackson Corners. Outside his window, the grass was long and brown and worn. And the kid was wrong.

LIAM GOT TIRED OF THE KID. He did. Things wore off, he got sober, and here was Kingston. He'd had enough. He gave Henry fare for the bus to Montreal, and begged off their deal. He doubled it, for food and whatnot. Now, Liam needed a room and some rest. He'd try the Skyway, he told the boy, who seemed concerned for Liam's well-being. The motel sat high off the Thruway, with a big sign, which they'd seen coming off the ramp, kind of a throwback to the time of motoring vacations—AIR CONDITIONED/COLOR TV.

But when Liam had said his good-byes at the little Trailways stop—he loved this kid, really, but where was the room to love another kid?—he pulled the Jeep back onto 87 North, and, with darkness sifting in, he felt free. He hooked his iPod into the sound system and found some Clifford Brown–Max Roach stuff, and tooled to the north.

These mile markers he had clicked off a thousand times— okay, perhaps a hundred, a handful of hundreds, but then he began to wonder: Could it be a thousand? No.

But it pleased him, as Clifford walked his kind of bright delicacy up and down the scales, that he'd established a beachhead for himself—what was he talking about, a beachhead! A mountain aerie, a retreat, rather, which he had never needed like he needed it now. Perhaps that was his plan. He'd go to the cabin. Yes, of course. He wasn't just driving aimlessly, was he?

His BlackBerry buzzed and he knew it was his wife. I'm gone, dear.

But he checked near Saugerties and it was an unrecognizable number and no message, so he pulled off to take a piss.

XIV

LIAM LOOKED NOT WITHIN HIMSELF but beneath—seated on the rest-stop toilet. His head down between his knees, he could see himself, his sad, sorry self, the essence of him—the he that had created his boy—his half of him—right there, the inverted turret, old, turtled or tortoised, a sad hide, hanging abjectly, in the dimness, waiting for water to come, looking down at the bowl, one blind eye: nothing.

He winced in the moment sometime after admiring his own thoughts and how they rolled themselves in language—for the length of one self-regarding glimpse at what he had just thought, he did admire his "inverted turret, old, turtled or tortoised, a sad hide"—the prosody of it, if you will. The inner rhymes, the assonance he'd once prided himself on—assonance mixed with alliteration—his specialty! But this gave way like an instant hangover to a recognition of cliché—musical, prosaic cliché—merely doing what a habitual blank-verse mind will do given English. He thought of an interview with Sonny Rollins in which Sonny recoiled at a playback of one of his famous improvised solos, shaking his head: Gotta delete the clichés, he said.

Liam wiped himself with a superfluity of care, for what was there to wipe, this older gent in a rest stop near Schroon Lake. He'd stopped for the hell of it, to see some light, to hear water run—light and water in the dark of night. And where is his son?

Back in the Jeep, the white stripe zipped under him like long laser salvos through his prostate, he could feel them, see them approaching one after another and feel their passage becoming a steady metronome of inner sound—my son, my son, my son, my son, my son, my son.

Where to, my son? Where from? Are you coming after me or am I coming to you? Are we both escaping? Have we escaped each other?

I am from here, Liam says aloud. And I am going home.

Where are you? What are you running from? Are you running? Have we left the world?

It is fucking cold. This fucking Jeep. Norwegian cold, Ibsen cold. Cold like that toilet was cold, the ring of the seat like ice. A throne of ice. Like John Gabriel Borkman, gripped by guilt and shame and defiance and ice. Like Borkman, his own sense of power—or was it freedom?—had ruined lives. And like Borkman, he is paying, and will forever pay until he enters some purification, some absolute zero of the soul, in ice.

He turns the radio on.

Perhaps it was a backfiring truck, they are now saying. No weapon, no shell casing, no bullet has yet been found. But several people fled—caught on the cameras. A young black man bolting through; an older black man shuffling off in a porkpie hat and sunglasses; a man of indeterminate race in a long brown raincoat, perhaps concealing something, as the day was warm in Kentucky; and the burly man in a tweed sport coat hurdling a police barrier.

The FBI was poring over footage and consulting security cameras surrounding the Riverwalk. "The investigation is ongoing and we have promising leads," says the man heading the investigation, a man who sounds like a bored southern bureaucrat.

Obama expresses no alarm and is noncommittal. "Listen folks, this is a dangerous job. As we know too well, public service is a dangerous job, for policeman, firemen—and women; our troops overseas and at home. And our politicians. It comes with the territory. I'm just sorry it spoiled a wonderful barbecue, and we'll be back to Paducah in due course."

It couldn't be Johnny, reasons Liam. It couldn't be. But

Liam trusts his eyes. Johnny, for some reason, was there, across the Indiana border into Kentucky. Why's that?

He waited for his phone to ring.

It was his wife. He'd pulled over to rest in the Dunkin' Donuts parking lot in Warrensburg. This was the end of his cell service going north. She was cool, if not cold. "I'm going to the cabin," he told her. "I'm working on a sequence about Borkman."

She said she hated the play. "Too stagy." She allowed as how she was going to work at home on the weekend and she'd arranged to have dinner with her "teacher," a gay fitness trainer. "I need to laugh."

Liam laughed, but he shouldn't have. It wasn't his cue. She hung up.

XV

LIAM'D RUN INTO A GUY AT THE TIN & LINT in Saratoga ten years ago now. It was a long night. He'd gone to the Spa to catch the races and meet a serious novelist from the region and talk about the writing life but had ended up having a long evening with locals. He thought he'd get a poem out of it at least—a friendly waitress showed him the booth where Don MacLean had written "American Pie," on a napkin, which the proprietor stuffed into MacLean's pocket as he was throwing the drunken guy out—when a chap sat down next to him at the corner post, where Liam was having his nightcap.

The fellow was a lush from a local paper company who'd always wanted to be a writer, but with the wife and kids etc., etc., and one thing led to another and they ended up somewhere else, and Liam let the man praise Liam's famous father-in-law's books and soon had the specs on a small bite of land on Lyon Mountain that Finch Pruyn Paper could excise from the deal with the Nature Conservancy, the guy would love to do it, it was a great place for a writer, he could tell, and he could make the call, and he was drunk—ten acres cleared, just a short walk up to the summit. "There's a spur from a fire road that leads right to it—it's a meadow. Thirty-five hundred feet. In the mornings you can walk to the summit in five minutes, see Canada. All the way. And the old man'll like it—how old is he?"

The house was an indulgence, yes—for a mountain shack, as his wife called it. She'd been once and the father-in-law never. But Liam, for all his efforts to leave behind his small-town upbringing, had nonetheless not left it, and it took an adulthood to realize this, as well as tens of thousands of dollars spent with Dr. Barton Frankel and others—that if he had any soul, it was here, in those mountains that loomed blackly to the north as he drove the smooth ribbon of the Northway. He knew right where he was going and hardly had to steer, such was the engineering of both this road and his spirit.

As the young Joyce told Mr. Ibsen, "a higher and holier enlightenment lies—onward."

He grabbed a Molson tallboy at the Stewart's in Warrensburg and some supplies—milk and cereal and fruit and a carton of Marlboros, why not. A box of matches, some C batteries. A case of Saranac IPA—Saranac, his homestead town, now with a brewery named after it that was 150 miles away.

Back on the highway, where in the dark he has for decades mulled his present, his future, plotted his moves, his career, it comes to him. Should this be Johnny involved in a shot on the president, he—the father—will become famous. The world will be curious about the poet/father of such a man; about the poet/father who left this boy's mother when the boy was three. About the poet/father of a would-be killer, the sensitive, thoughtful verse maker. The world would eagerly await his take on this tragic turn; would feast, perhaps, on the shame he must feel, his guilt; would savor his reflections in words upon the experience. Tell us what it means, Liam Brogan. You, above all people, will know.

He wished he'd brought fresh blades with him, but then considered that the grizzled look would suit the occasion, should it arise. A cabin interview, say.

He thinks of a poem he's abandoned that, with a few tweaks, would be read as prophetic.

Liam sees a hitchhiker at the end of the entrance ramp at exit 25. It couldn't be Henry, could it? He motors past.

He's punished himself enough. This is his counsel. He's punished himself physically, mentally, financially with increasing intensity over the last three decades. Johnny was his mistake—his great mistake: a child from an early marriage of passion and drugs and alcohol and dreams of rebellion. How unfair. How bourgeois. How 1970s to think that rebellion on this level was a coherent personal statement— that he was saying something. Years of therapy and reading had given him many "insights," views into theories of what would explain away his many mistakes. One, he was trying to emulate his birth mother, who gave him up, and thereby exonerate her by matching her in his own abandonings—a way not to hate her (Dr. Lipton). Two, because of his adoption, he did not understand family and tried his best to build family in the dark, and could not be blamed for getting it wrong (Dr. Solow). Three, by being "chosen" by his adoptive parents, he understood he could always be unchosen, making all relationships contingent, and allowing him to treat family in similar terms, as something that could be tried and left. After all, he'd adapted, why couldn't they? (Dr. Frank). Four, a mixture of all: Unable to blame or hate his mother (a woman he did not know), he did not understand the bonds of family, and thought all relationships were contingent, and this is what he tried to teach his own child, as if he were a miner consigning his own son to the same life in the mines (D. H. Lawrence). But he loved his son.

He'd have to work on that; it was hardly a sound bite.

He'd have to step on it to get ice and firewood and propane in Plattsburgh.

JOHNNY HAD ALL HIS PROBLEMS, and more. He'd bounced from woman to woman, too; he drank. He'd also done a stint in prison—bar fight, assault. Still on probation, Liam imagined, though he didn't stay abreast of all such developments.

Loved the kid, but done him wrong. No doubt, the kid believed that. There was no rinsing it out. It was something that could, at best, be lived with, not removed like some stain. It was there, and that was one of Liam's greatest mistakes, to think such things would fade. After being surrendered by his own birthing mother a few hours after she'd housed him for nine months, all was forgotten, expunged—it was even expunged from the public record, not to mention an infant's memory. Sort of. "I guess that's what we're talking about," Liam said to the self of him reflected back in his windshield, his glasses with dashboard rubies glinting. He swerved around some roadkill and was shocked to see his first moose standing there on the shoulder, a big rack and chest set high on the ladder of his legs. Liam pulled over, got out, and then panicked. He had a beer can open and he'd been drinking since morning, but Bullwinkle loped off across the lanes into the wooded median anyway, so Liam got back in the Jeep and roared off, his heart pounding so that a stitch beneath his left pectoral throbbed. He was sure this is how he would die one day—infarction.

There was the necessary stop in Plattsburgh and he made it. There was no need to rush; he'd forgotten—you could get propane at the twenty-four-hour Sunoco station, and ice, and packs of "camp wood." He picked up a couple of cold ones for the forty-five minutes more he had to go.

Liam was fearless about the drinking and driving, if he wasn't coming out of some tavern establishment. Regular citizens going to and from upstate weren't subject to being stopped unless they were weaving or racing, and there were no troopers on the back roads anyway, so he was safe, safe to relax with a can between his legs, sipping, relaxing, spacing out the ride with thoughts of elsewhere. The final leg of it all went smoothly, and when he made it to the edge of his property in the total darkness, his headlights frighting the pines around him, all he wanted to do was dive inside, find the bed, whack it a few times, light the Coleman, see what he'd been reading last time he was here, and fade away.

A movie screening in a dark, private theater, with couches. Watching with a team of filmmakers—their film—and a few of their friends. Liam doesn't personally know any of them. At first, he is seated next to the choreographer, who seems gay. They share a couch. As the film begins, Liam mentions to him that over there is Alan Good—a dancer he's seen in the Merce Cunningham troupe. Oh, gushes the choreographer, Yes, he was simply brilliant in *Showboat*. Did you see *Showboat*? No, says Liam, laughing. Just the Cunningham company. I don't think I'd go see *Showboat*. The choreographer leaves in a huff. Then a young Russian woman slides in next to Liam. He knows her name, somehow—Valdaya. She has large head, big green eyes, and a small body. She must be a dancer, he thinks. Valdaya is very friendly, and puts her hand on his chest expressively, very familiar. Liam thinks about cheating on his wife. Someone discreetly appears to take a drink order in a whisper. Liam doesn't know what to have. He is distracted. Valdaya says, "I'll have a Guinness." Then, Liam doesn't want to have a Guinness; it would appear to be copying her, trying to impress, ingratiate. But he genuinely loves Guinness. He says, "A Guinness." Valdaya says to him, "'A Guinness,'" in a low growl, imitating him, her green eyes lifted toward him over a thin grin. He wakes up.

The cabin is bright with light. There is snow in the field all around, which he'd hardly noticed when he pulled in. Perhaps it had snowed during the night. It had; there are no tracks from the car to the front porch, upon which he now stands, shivering. The sunlight reflects bright sheets off the snow and fills the windows with white light, and the two small rooms inside. He goes back in, and he can hardly see for a moment and he closes his eyes. He sees in his mind's eye the tweed coat hanging over the back of a chair, and when he opens his eyes, it is there.

In his earlier days, Liam was part of a literary community—short-lived but real. Poets, artists, dancers, spiritual adventurers. If there was an idea holding it together, it was a belief that the imagination could transform reality. This was practiced and pursued and found in many ways—the poetry of Blake and Coleridge, the writing of Goethe, Hegel, Nietzsche, Owen Barfield; and even the deconstructionists, who saw that reality was transformed by systems of expression, detrimentally.

To Liam, at first, it was hocus-pocus, no different from his childhood Catholicism: Your belief becomes reality. But he soon learned that the act of imagining could release to the surface realities within, which then could be incorporated into the reality without, changing it. Drugs and drink and reading did this for him; meditation; going places in his mind and coming back with something; dreams.

His father-in-law had claimed that "fiction is an epistemology, a system of knowing." The same thing.

Liam didn't really buy it, after a while. He put it down—his own efforts in life could not change anything or anyone, certainly not himself, or his son, or his marriages, or his career. But now he sat at the little square pine kitchen table in a chair opposite the draped tweed coat from Dublin that he'd bought for himself and given his son and seen on television the day before. Where'd that come from?

He'd wait. His son was here.

There was no need for the radio. Liam realized he already knew more than the world.

He forgot about his own little poems, his moment in the harsh limelight. This was real.

Had he conjured something out of the dark? Was he in the true realm of art and faith after all, after all his living? Was this wisdom? If his son would come, he would know. And he would wait.

There was no clock ticking, but the cabin did—it ticked as it settled and adjusted in the wind blowing off the mountain, and did so with a regularity, as if calibrated.

The morning wore on and the headache burned itself out. Liam began to feel clean. He sat at the table with his palms out before him on the comforting pine boards. With his hands flat and his haunches in the chair and wool-stockinged feet grabbing the floor, he had the sensation he was strapped into a moment in time or space—both—captaining himself atop a long sinew of incident, accident, and science that extended to the core of things, through the floor and the shallow cellar and into the anorthosite upon which this structure was built, down through miles of it to where there were only canyons of lightless magma. He shivered at the thought, but pleasantly, as if part of a universal fascia that was firing everywhere in this blessed moment fired in him.

He held this feeling, captured it with his mind like a wild raven in his hands and then set it free. It flew, but tethered to him by the very logic to which he was tethered to all. It rose above him—or he grew, elevated, through the crossbeams and latticework, the shingles and the chimney flashing and the chimney stones themselves into the network of air, the atmosphere really, past the surrounding pines, in which he could see, now below him, a raven's nest, and then on past the cliff face, gray and wet, and to the bald summit with its two scraggly pines, wind-battered to hat racks of brown needles; and he could see the valley flowing west to Upper Chateaugay like an embroidered train, and beyond, to the St. Lawrence plain and its shimmering silver vein and out there, past that, Canada. Through the forests he could see his son trekking to him, breathing heavily, wandering, lost, looking for his coat, or his father, or something to eat or drink, laboring in a nimbus of his breath, looking for his mother, somewhere, frozen in the turf, her face peaceful, at repose; for the look of love for a grieving son she'd abandoned, he was looking.

All this, but here only an empty coat. Had hours passed? There was little light left, but what there was shot through the low window over the sink and across from Liam, above the lintel, the thin light splashed and danced a line. Words threatening to form, as they had when he was young and fooled with the psychotropics and he'd read distinctly a script in the clouds that he knew and recognized but could not recall or make plain after; here, on the lintel, a line drew out, in gold and orange, four, five, six clusters, forming and re-forming but holding a certain syntax, an orthography, six signs or words. He peered hard from many angles of view, though he remained in place. He saw this: *Fall in love.* He saw *Fall in love*—it came clear and held—*with what is.* With what is held; and that was that. A cliché to be deleted, per Sonny Rollins? Oh, it held, and he thought for a pen. He had no pen and he did not want to move, but leaned across—Johnny'd have one in the coat. Indeed he did—Liam's own Parker pen, a gift to him from—for crissakes, Christmas. Two months ago. He wrote on the deal table the phrase: *Fall in love with what is.* And then began to panic. What the fuck is this?

That is to say, what is?

And how to love it?

Liam recognized nothing about the space he was in; he realized that he could not say what day it was, only that it was winter. Surely, he could cipher it out, given a little thought, but he surrendered instead to the drift, and resisted sending his mind back to an identifiable date and then marching forward on a hunt for today and nail it. No, he stayed suspended, and the panic, which had gripped his diaphragm, released. He did recognize something, though, about his location in another kind of landscape. He had often in his work found himself right here—at the summit of something, or very near it, having made a certain journey, excitedly, pleasurably, with passion and commitment, as if he were running somewhere he would recognize when he reached it, always only to end up like here, lost, unable to go on or get back down or go home. Not for the first time had he written himself into an impasse—in this case, an empty two-room cabin. He'd done this sort of thing a hundred times, and here he was again, but somehow with a talisman of what he had given away, draped over a chair.

Somewhere out there was his son. He'd be back any minute; he had to be. The night was coming on—the whole day had nearly passed, and it was beginning to snow and blow. The cabin had given up ticking off its seconds and what he heard now was a long, unmistakable moan. Him.

Finishing Ulysses

Y OU STAND IN THE MIRROR. Cheeks smart, from the shave.
Your blue eyes wander—hooded, you'd say, but that will
change. These'll wake you up. You swallow two without water,
then rinse your mouth. Thinning a bit, right there. And you
missed a spot—the hollow beneath your lip. Look like Diz.

Take stock: Two is a world away from one. This apropos
your pack of smokes. You tap your second-to-last out of the
pack into your left hand and put it to your mouth. One
remains. The pack rattles assuredly. You think that—you
know *assuredly* is not right: *assuringly* is, but you like the *d*
rattling around in the pack, that sound. Words have body.
Should. "Cut the thread but leave the whole heart whole."
Lorenz Hart. *Whole heart whole*—what is that . . . diastole.
Heart and soul, right there. Funny: Hart/heart. Homophone.

Back in your shirt pocket. Five is close to four, so close,
hardly a difference. Four is close to three, and three to two.
But two is a world away from one. Exactly. One left, eternal
supply. In reserve, never without one. Good name for a tune.

You finish your smoke, surprised in the rising steam of
the hot tap you left running that you see an image of yourself as a boy, your young eager face in the lower right of the
glass, looking up. It's Marion there with your baby son—
your new son.

—You been in here a while, Bob. You okay? I'm putting him to bed.

Looks more like her, you think.

—You look beautiful, you say. This is the thing, the real thing, doll. The home. You say brightly, My Penelope.

Marion withdraws from the bathroom, from you, with a shy smile. She trusts you are happy, that's all. On the way now to the big family, not as big as yours was—she can't do that. And she knows you don't want that—no ten kids. Soon, you'll be writing for the *News*. And this is your house. You'll pay for it.

—When are you back, Bob? Not too late.

You square your shoulders, tug the lapels. Down the steps like lightning like Gene Kelly to the living room, you don your tweed cap at the door and touch Marion's cheek and the boy's.

—Not too late, you say. A couple of sets downtown, me and Jimmy Curran.

Get a wobble on the sidewalk, but you straighten it out and decide the stride is right, then left along a central axis and that's the balance you need and have, all there. Guy Rodgers down the lane switching hands, you even bend over a bit in hoopster style; your one smoke flips on the stones, stopping you. Out comes your Ronson, that decisive metallic click and the blue flame wavers there—no it doesn't: *click, click, click,* there. Odor still: Korea, '47. That wasn't so bad. Indelible imprint, though, but a smell. But fuck Ike running again. You exhale the blue jet. Longest day of the year. Just past, what was it: last Thursday.

Hey, funny: Rodgers, then Hart.

Need flints.

You pick up the pace and wonder at the heat. Rain due. Hustle. Take it on the arches.

Crazy, man, and you head for Pat's up at Broad and Erie. Smokes you need and why not the bennies. Some jump. Setting sun crashing into the facade of the church over there. Not crashing. What? Spilling down. Glazing.

Glazing. Bronze and gold, enameling: Yeats. No no. Mina Kennedy and whatshername. Ormond Hotel.

Douce, Lydia. And the flints.

Not Ike. Why you thinking Ike? He can't beat your guy. No more wars. You got boys. Boy. But you'll have boys in due course. At least: You'd be exempt. No you wouldn't. Ted fucking Williams. What's he hitting?

I don't have time for baseball.

—There's the good Pat; how's the cat?

—Bobby the hipster, how's the scene? You mokes, where ya been? your brother asks you, rubbing your head.

You duck and laugh. He's made his way, a druggist. How convenient.

—How's the paperboy's business?

—Hot, you tell him, because it is. You canvass for ads. You could be Bloom. But it's still a dig; you both know it: New York.

The little envelope. Pat knows the drill. Flints, yep. Two packs of Old Gold. House account, you say, to a grunt. Little brother discount.

The evening paper.

—Give us this day our daily press, you intone to the bemused newsdealer, Charlie Black. You thumb-flash it open, sheets hissing. Right there. You needed the right-hand position. Let's see. Did Murray get it? He did. Not bad: That's thirty-two sixty-five, your pocket.

Good you came back. Yes.

There's Dave.

—Hey. Fuckin' Brogan, how are ya? Dave says he's good and he's got a house for you. Give him a call. Over in Oak Lane.

—Brogan, you tell him—nice car he's got, that Pontiac— can't move out of the Kid.

—Understand, Bob. But we're all fleeing the parish.

—Hey hey, you yell as he waves and slaps the hot green door boom boom. How's Ginny?

He doesn't hear and just as well. He doesn't know; that's right.

That's right: Sam's. Jimmy Curran there. Catch him with his cherry Coke a doke you singsong. Five cents. The Jewish guys drink the three-center, seltzer only, no syrup. Smart really. Like you: You've got your flask. Little Fleischmann's in.

You see Sam there. These are the good guys, solid. Great neighbors, right on the edge of the Kid. Lucky. The Irish'd never think of a soda fountain. Who's here?

Crazy, for a Monday night. Game on CAU.

—Who's pitching? you ask McCoy. As if you care. As if he knows.

—Robby, Solly Feister pipes up. You actually like Robin Roberts—son of a Welsh coal miner. Lives in Gwynedd Valley. Or should. Should win twenty again too.

—Solly, what's shaking? you say.

—You, if you ask me. And you did. What's Irish up to tonight?

—Waiting on my acolyte. You might not capisce, what am I saying?

—Little Jimmy.

—He's in the back, plugging a nickel in the Wurlitzer.

—Good they fired fucking Herman the Red, big voice booms in. Who the— You see Big Mick squat over the red stool and spread his shit.

—Ya, excuse me, you say, not budging. He wobbles, the plastic groans, but he's not moving.

—Gimme a cherry Coke, Sam. And a Danish. Now what's wrong with the rebel Robert Emmet Doherty? He sniffs, like he could deduce.

—I don't know that anything's wrong. I'm standing here.

—Sam, says Big Mick. His jowls jiggle like there's small rodents shifting around. Herman Beilan, he bellows. One of yours, Sam? Gotta be.

—That I don't know. That's fifteen cents. Want a straw?

—He was a Commie, so you know I figured: Hebrew persuasion. And a teacher! Hey Bob, you fought the slopeheads over there. We lost guys—the McGonigle brothers, you remember those guys. Good yiddance, I say.

He slurpslops his Danish.

—Here's the lad, you say. Good Jimmy Curran. He needs some assuring, that look. Nothing's wrong but this—you swing your head down the counter and Jimmy gets the drift: moving.

—Nothing's wrong, you say, taking advantage of the shuffle to spill a little Fleishshmann's in your seltzer. But this bum, a bigot.

—Like the Citizen, Bob, right. Like the Citizen at Davy Byrne's.

—The Ormond, Jimmy. No, Barney Kiernan's. Got to get there someday. Yeah, like the Citizen whose name you know what his name was it was Cusack, Michael Cusack. Based on. What they say, I can't say who, just general knowledge now, Jimmy, there's a lot for you to read, but the book's the place to start and finish. Do you want something? Sam! Jimmy here'll have . . .

—You know Nora Brogan over there in, you know, Dave and Ginny and Anne and Joan, all those nice honeys, you're familiar, eh? Their mother was a Cusack. A real gem, that woman. Mayo, I think.

—Are they all still in New York, was it Anne and Virginia, and your old steady, Cassie, was it?

Our Citizen here—you realize from Jimmy's daft look he's not following this; you have that problem: You talk too fast—this fucker's just after having himself a little speech about Commie Jews, you repeat. Fuck him. Bad as McCarthy. Sam should put some jizz in his Danish.

—I don't know what they're doing, you say, putting a quarter on the counter. Out of the Kid all I know.

You wander out into the night—not really night yet. You can hear the crowd at Shibe Park roar as warmth and breeze touch you. Radio roar. Ashburn, probably. Still some sunlight. A fair June day, you announce; then you shiver. What did Joyce say: reminder of the chill grave that awaits you. Some such thing. You could ask Jimmy. He wouldn't know, too young for it all.

—It is a nice day, Bob, says Jimmy Curran trailing you as you head to the subway a little farther down Broad Street.

Nothing matters, nothing is. Here you are mid-swim—can you swim? Good thing, that pull on Coney Island. Great-uncle never made it—grandfather's brother, drowned on the hottest day of the year. Nineteen thirty-eight. Charlie.

Walking underground, safer maybe. False lights and the smell of death. Rats, natural causes. No removal. Jimmy's quiet. You hate to talk down here, only think. Bad luck, like chatting in a crypt. You feel a rivulet of sweat go down your spine. Smoke, why not. Old Gold. Tear the pack. Click.

You know this confusion. It's your thrill. Those trills, running through the changes like Bird. Up and down the scales, fast fingering and blow, blow, blow and breathe. Joyce wrote before jazz, imagine that. None of that prose inflected. Shakespeare wrote before the dictionary. Joyce before Bean or Prez. No Diz. And yet, riverrun, the Wake. Talk about running through the changes. He knew. Had a beautiful voice. McCormack.

Shoulda heard more in New York, 'stead of chasing James T. Farrell around. But Philly's got it now, man. Now can afford, too. What'd you give. Up. Not the poet, you can learn. Out and dig it. Half the world—our own Dick Clark. Abomination. He should go to the Zanzibar. See how heroin dances—still, very still.

The soft gong sound felt in *philadelphia*. Nice, that. Make a note of it.

Jimmy's quiet. He knows. Schooling him. Here we are, you say, and you hike up to the street at Columbia.

—Music City, baby, you tell him. Hey, it's Monday; there'll be a short jam. Always is.

Jimmy's got his battered copy. There'll be questions. But let's listen; that's your idea. Up the steps, at Seventeenth and Chestnut. Second floor. Already warming up, you can hear it as you climb, a sweet trumpet. Lee Morgan?

And there you are. Tollin already at the kit. Piano you don't recognize. Ziggy Vines with the tenor. Don't know bass.

Brownie on horn!

—Jimmy, you say. In for a treat.

A good crowd standing around, in the aisles. You might

pick something up. Max Roach and Clifford together now. Get that one. Maybe later.

You find a spot, near a bin you can lean on. You could use a drink. Pep's later. You can sneak Jimmy in there if Satch is at the door.

You're late. But looks like Brownie's just stepped in. Kind soul. Clean as a whistle, they say. Loves chess, doesn't drink. Or smoke. Amazing. Wilmington kid. Math whizz. You recognize that—Gillespie tune. "Night in Tunisia."

In the next five minutes you leave your body. Everyone's soul leaves and mingles in the air of the shop. Brownie—you've never heard anyone like him. Quick, fast, assured, buttery, bright notes finger every vertebrae in your spine up then down then right to your brain stem and a rapid tapping across your scalp and your temples tingle and that's when you leave, every note unexpected yet perfectly placed, as if it could only be that note but you don't know what the note should be till he hits it and then you knew it a second before and that's why it's perfect, like life, predictable mysteries, the continuity of life, blowing, a hundred thousand repeated breaths, each different but absolutely necessary and a must. And people are jiving, yeah, Brownie, yeah, go, Brownie, and he leaves off and Ziggy actually steps in, and listen to him, he learned a few things right there, the coloration, the tone and that little trick there, a Clifford Brown signature he just stole, that's okay. From the best. Don't rob a pauper, but a prince. And yes, Ziggy, nice hand, and Brownie, he's gonna take us out, and out, not before holding a note, holds it like a wild bird in the bell of his horn and then he lets it go, a bright flight soars off and away and quiet. Then you erupt, back in your body, the sweat pouring off Brownie's round creased face; you can see the button he's built on his lip, a homely friendly-looking face. Speaking now, a soft chocolaty voice. Thank you, he says. Thank you for making me feel so wonderful. Thanking us! It's so hot, he says, and laughs softly, and man he is right—hot licks, hot Philly. He's gotta go.

You've got to go too, you're hyperventilating near, and maybe it's the pills, but you think it's the something else that's firing every nerve like you are a live wire, an open socket, and you and Jimmy zip down the steps and you stand there on Chestnut, breathing. Beadilybeadillybeadily deet-deet, deedily beady deet, beadily deet deet deedle eet be down, done, done down, too done, to do—bright bright bleat. Your head shaking, you're trying something.

—Let's down to Pep's. South Broad. We'll walk. Jimmy's a little nervous. Not our neighborhood, you hear him say. And it is mostly dark cats moving about, club to club, joint to joint, some just standing around. But it's cool enough. Phillies game in the air from somewhere, all can relate. Well, some. Talk along the way, calm him down.

—That right there, you say—that's jazz, man. It's a new kind of storytelling. Where does it go? It goes around and around itself and builds itself each time—eights and eights and eights and eights back to the head and out. Imagine telling a story like that! Not just one long thin note, point a to point b. Not just moving a sand pile from one place to another. Building a fucking castle, man, out of pecans, and bring everyone there, stopping by everywhere and people get on, picking people up, rounding 'em up for a tour of the castle.

Jimmy's quiet after all that. He bums a smoke off you. Contemplative. A deep kid. A reader, and not many of them in the parish. You know, so you walk.

Ghosts all about. It was Korea, read *Portrait* going over. Converted some to the church, that speech Joyce cribbed from some parish bull. Put you off—out of the church. Jimmy's headed that way, too, his mother told you. To your face. You've put him off the church, Robert Doherty. Some call that the devil, I want you to know.

Thanks, Mrs. Curran. And God bless.

Sufficient unto the day is the evil thereof.

The kid wants more and it's good for you, you think. Running through all the stations, of your . . . disbelief.

There's Pep's. Down, and, indeed, Satch at the door. Chet Baker on the bill, a good crowd. Prefer standing at the bar anyway, cheaper, buck fifty Schmidt's. Long wait, time to talk.

In the bathroom, Gerry Mulligan, hometown boy. Baritone. Making it. Handsome fucking guy.

—Hey, Gerry, you say. Here to see Chet?

—Of course, fella, he says to you. The long urinal trough sings and smells. Just saw Brownie at Ellis Tollin's, you tell him.

—Gonna see him in California, Gerry says. He and Roach are recording out there, you know. Nice sound. They're shaking it up. Hard hop to it, but Max can do anything. And this kid. Wow.

—Smart cats, you say.

—Righto, says Mulligan. You see he's high as a kite, mishandling his own zipper. One thing at a time.

—Cool, you say, and leave him be.

You rub your hands, returning to the bar, where Jimmy guards your two glasses of beer. A good view from there, if you can hold it.

Jimmy leans in and tells you softly what's on his mind. He's having trouble. You have to ratchet back to where you might have been, always a problem, but then you understand he's talking about Joyce. He's trying to understand, but he doesn't understand.

—What happened? you ask, knowing.

—Bob, it's the greatest book I've ever read, by a million miles—nothing like it, nothing near as good—for a while. Then I honestly don't know what's going on. Or what happens. Tell me: What happens?

—I told you to take it slow, you tell him.

There's a long lull. Sound checks, the crowd stirs. You turn your attention to the little bandstand along the back wall. Chet's got three horns standing there. But then the stage is emptied and it's back to the merry concert of ice clinking and throaty laughter and a cash register chunking open and closed and running water. Warm sounds you think are the height of civilization now in peace-time. That's all Ike needs, face it. Prosperity in the heartland and scenes like this in the cities. It's good. Good enough for people to think it's good anyway. Narcotic.

—I'll tell you what, you say to Jimmy. I'm gonna teach a course. I talked to my guy at Temple, big Joyce fan, old Gordo, a scholar, I've told you. I told him I had an idea; he said work it up. I could actually teach part-time, GI extension, like it would be a seminar or something. Little extra scratch for me and Marion.

—I'd sign up, Jimmy says.

—This is it, I'll tell you then. Course called "Finishing *Ulysses*."

—That would help!

—No no no, you explain. It's like this: course description, student reads the title, "Finishing *Ulysses*," says, That's for me, I'll finally finish that fucking book! But that's not what it is. Student reads on: the prerequisite is this—now dig this—you have to have read the book at least twice already, class size is whatever Temple wants. But students don't get in if on the first day they can't answer five questions about the book. Get four outta five, you're out. Right there, slip of paper. Five-minute class. In or out.

Jimmy looks nervous. What to say, you know he's wondering. What kind of questions?

—Okay: One. What day of the week is Bloomsday? Two. What's the name of the priest who presides at Paddy Dignam's funeral?

—I know that one; it's a pun, Jimmy says. Conmee, he comes up with, Father Conmee?

—Nope. Close. Three: What odds did Throwaway pay?

Bored now you are.

—Et cetera, Jimmy. You'll get in, don't worry . . . if your mommy allows for your further corruption.

You feel odd for a moment as you realize you've not told this idea to anyone other than professor Gordo over a brief pint and you're telling it to a seventeen-year-old and so what if you convince him, but that's not the issue, why isn't your circle something else. You can tell this to Red Murray down at the *News*. Try this on Larry Merchant? But you carry on. The eagerness of a young son is more than enough. You go on.

—This is what we do and it addresses the very problem you are having right now, Jimmy. All we read in this class is the first six chapters. The three of Stephen's and the three of Bloom's, takes both of them from about eight till eleven on Bloomsday, breakfast to funeral. Dedalus goes and picks up his pay, walks the strand. They are beautiful; you are right. Nothing like it before or since. Ineluctable modality of the visible. Signatures of all things I am here to read.

—Yes, yes, says Jimmy. Wavewhite wedded words shimmering on the dim tide.

—He's got a bright light on. And he follows these guys around, this Odysseus, and this son, this, what, Telemachus. They are wandering and of course their paths must cross; they must find each other. Father and son. That's the odyssey, isn't it. Coming home, Odysseus home to Penelope and his boy. Stephen's lost his mother, hasn't he. He sees her at sea. His father is an earache. Did you see that Bloom has to share a carriage with the old man Dedalus to Glasnevin? Question four: Who's in the carriage with Bloom?

—But I tell you what I think—why the whole book changes. Episode seven, Aeolus. Something breaks there and it gets more broken—he goes further and further from writing a novel. He's writing about something else. He's writing about the novel or writing itself, not these guys' stories. He's interested in how bad the novel is as a form. An English invention and he's a good Irishman. He hates the English and their ways. Hated Dublin, too, but it was in his blood. So what's he do? I think he couldn't stomach carrying out the plot where, you know, A meets B. Stephen meets Bloom; then what? A contrivance. Or worse. I really think Joyce saw the conventional novel like a form of imperialism. Abuses circumstance, abuses mystery, in favor of . . . imposing a story. Rewriting maps, borders. Eliminates. I mean, people fart in *Ulysses*.

—So what does Joyce do, that's the point. He looks for a resolution, what Gordo called a formal resolution. Aesthetic. He leaves off any pretense to having this turn out to be a story with an ending that has a beginning. It is a novel that had a beginning and a novel that finds an ending as a novel, not as a story. As a collection of words. He's got these people looking for people and they're not going to find them. Bloom—his

dead son; his lost father. Stephen—his lost mother; a real
father. His father's dead to him. At the end, what? Stephen
walks off into the night. Where's he go? Bloom crawls into
bed, where old Blazes Boylan had been not too goddamned
long ago. Maybe he gets breakfast in bed tomorrow. Fat
chance. Thing is, Joyce doesn't give a fuck about the narrative development after's he's set up a big map. Happy endings
are not his business. He wants to get everything in instead.
Circumstance, like I said. Mystery. The whole world of a day.

The mike shrieks with feedback and some guy in a suit
announces to boos that Chet Baker can't make it tonight
and you see that Mulligan has already split from his table
and taken the dame with him. And some other musicians
are stirring in and will set up, but the dissent lasts only a
moment and back to the tinkling set and the barkeep, Al
Parker, says to you, Bob, this round's on the house. But not
the shots. Good luck.

—So this is it, you go on, blowing through your own stop
sign. If you make the class and get your five right then you
have to finish writing *Ulysses*. Finish *Ulysses*, and turn it in at
the end of term; I don't want to see you till then. Your first six
chapters are written for you. You find a resolution on whatever level, and you decide, and argue in a short paper, how
you resolved it and how you think Joyce resolved it or didn't
resolve it. That's it. What do you think?

—There's Jim Doyle. Right there. Near the Yuengling sign.
Ask him, Bob.

—Doyle knows, you say. Get him over here.

Your other Jimmy friend. At Temple now after the merchant marines. Wants to be a playwright.

—Doyle, you say. You love this guy, got a twinkle like
Spencer Tracy.

—Just telling Jimmy here about my theory—yeah, Chet Baker's canceled; let's just visit, eh. Seeing Doyle's heavy coat. Is it, starting to rain? All the more reason. You call Al over for another round and settle Jim Doyle in. On his own. Reading Ibsen, you see, in his CPO coat pocket.

—Doyle here doesn't buy it, right, Jim? Too much the playwright, but it's an interesting point. Tell him, you say.

Doyle's a reticent friend, and the way you can talk, that's a particular disadvantage. But he's careful and knows what he thinks and what he thinks he is not afraid to tell you.

—Joyce aspired to the theater, he tells you. Wrote one play but was headed there again, maybe didn't know it. But *Ulysses* ends in performance, a verbal performance—an orgasm, of course—but it is a monologue, a great one, Molly coming to yes. A fifth of the book is a play, with stage directions. Nighttown. An impossible piece to stage, for obvious reasons—and never in Dublin! And it's the perfect ending, the only ending, brings it all full circle. The book finds home, the omphalos, even if Bloom and Dedalus don't. That's my view. Believe me, Bob, he tells you, those students of yours will do no better.

—You see, you say to Jimmy Curran. It will make for great debate. And Doyle here—he's made my class. If he wants to . . . I'll feed you the answers, my two Jameses, you say.

You wink at him and you all toast.

—Maybe that's right, Jimmy Curran says, looking at Doyle but talking to you. This book is done, let's study it, not finish it. Happened what, fifty years ago. Before the wars, before the Republic even.

There's another round from Al Parker, the beer, the whiskey. That kind of night. If fucking Chet Baker had kept his nose clean, it'd be different. You recognize what's happening—getting a little surly—but you can control it.

Jimmy Curran speaks up. I just don't know that it works, he tells you. It's not a novel is all I'm saying.

—Curran, you're a little young for this, don't you think? Bedtime. He's immediately hurt. You punch his shoulder and smile. You can kid a kid, you say. He relaxes, but he looks at his watch. Doyle shifts closer, moving into the space you've just contested a little. A Jim Doyle move. Last thing you want is a fight at sea. Peacekeeper.

—Let me say this, you say—as if you ever have had to claim the floor, your gift, to be the youngest and everybody doted on what you had to say, those still around anyway. Hey now. Look at *Dubliners*. Every story tight as a fucking drum. Sight, see it right, the right voice, you say—poof: epiphany. Every one of 'em. A secret formula taken from the Bible. Joyce probably puked his fucking guts out when he realized that.

—Bob, Bob, says Jim. Now slow down.

Slow down, boys, huh? You say, It's fucking raining, it's a fucking Monday night, the blues, and we are in Philadelphia and I got a house I owe on and a new kid and a job selling ads, so I'm firing through this right now. C'mon, this is interesting. If not, fuck off.

You excuse yourself with some courtesies and go to the jakes, leak and one to take the edge off the whiskey, which has made you ugly, you know, and you are sorry for it. Pissing, you remember standing next to Dylan Thomas in the White Horse and you look there like you could conjure him here in Pep's and you can't and you remember Ginny and Cassie making fun of you: Be a poet; don't chase one. Thanks a lot. Hoofers.

You wrote for Hallmark, six months. Okay.

They were something. Not hoofers, sirens, yours. In the white tile in front of you, you see Ginny Brogan's face in that geisha routine she did. Cabaret. In the Village. Rubber-band eyes. What'd she. . . . Adorable.

Back to the bar and you hate to tell Jimmy it's time to go, but he's reloaded his question. Beer to his head. It doesn't work, he says. The book. I don't know what it is.

—Look, you say. A book about identity is entitled to have some identity problems of its own: it should. I think Joyce resolved it. As much as a book with a ghost in it can be resolved.

—Let's go.

It's raining hard now, but it feels good after a long hot June. The streets are sloshing; your feet are wet. Jimmy's in Keds. Doyle, you say to Doyle, well shod. You look at his bruised rib-soled deck shoes from the good ship *Lollipop*. You think, Grossbooted drayman.

—Let's down to the Z Bar, you say. Mulligan said Prez might show up. You lie, but it's strategic—keep these pals moving; it's too early. Life is good; there's air to breathe.

Your smoke is wet in the rain and you have to piss again, but the Zanzibar is closed—some Mondays, that's right. Doyle knows Mulligan told you no such thing and you don't hide behind the lie—there's enough of that ahead—and Doyle steers you and Jimmy back down the street and across to a small shop surrounded by *News* trucks: delivery guys, bringing the paper up, early edition. What the hell time is it—2:00 A.M. by the Bulova. How can that be? You grab a copy from the back and put it back—there's a stack inside the shop and a coffee would be good right now and you can take the paper home to Marion, businesslike; she'll be worried. Tuesday's coupons.

You try to catch up with where you are in the little mop closet you have to take a piss in—micturition, of course. You're a nation after all, unto yourself. And it is always thus. You can hear the two Jims out there lightly conversing and you know that is not a part of you; you are always your own consuming fire, one big hearth aflame, and sometimes people gather and sometimes people don't and you can't see out anyway; mighty Casey has struck out—like you're in the klieg lights themselves, blind to the audience, you can only talk and talk as you hear things. You sit down in there. You sit down in a mop closet in Bud's diner in the middle of Philadelphia USA and the rest of the world could dissolve, imagine it—the last closet standing, you exit to a ruined world. Then: mop up. You decide to smoke and think, and you can hear Ginny, or is it Cassie—really no matter—saying, What's wrong, Bobby? Settle down. Look at yourself. What do you want. Drive you fucking crazy. You toss the butt. What are you doing? Sweet Marion's face.

You look at the poem in your pocket. Almost lost in the lining, so you have to dig.

> *Deep in my heart's well, fluffed and grey,*
> *The ashes of love no longer smolder,*
> *When fanned they glowed and sparked a bit*
> *But soon went out and now grow colder.*

Gray and *bit* don't work.

> *Old Bob less love was incomplete;*
> *New Bob of others joys will take,*
> *What if till then my heart skips a beat?*
> *I think the drink was worth the ache.*

Really, you think. Is it worth it? And what do you want? See your son. You should go home. Should have named him

William, like in the book—William Doherty, D.D. Call him Liam. Maybe she. No. Not hers to name.

Not Tim, after your da. Not after him. Loss and guilt, all that unites them, the very only thing . . . is what?

Kevin. Kevin Barry's good.

Scrap that poem. But: back in your pocket. You wipe, your tail burning.

The light in the counter area is blinding. One napkin dispenser burns like phosphorus. The fire you are in. Jim and Jimmy are at a back table, three coffees. Who's the guy who just left? you ask. No, this one's for you, says Doyle. No, you say. Someone just left. Someone just went somewhere, you say, looking through the plate-glass window. You realize "bud" in reverse is "bud"—obverse.

You sit down. Somebody just left, you mutter. The seat seems warm. Its seams are warm, or is it the piping, and you get a chill; you shiver up through your tweed cap. You look at the newspaper—the consolations of print, its warm assurances, the many points of purchase, you claim them, one after another, climb around in the typography, and you realize you are reading a little item that says Clifford Brown is dead. Turnpike, rain-slicked, a turn. Two others. You can't fucking believe it. You saw Brownie, what, six hours ago. Rain-slicked. A turn. Turnpike.

You don't say anything, because this can't be true.

—Robert Emmet buried by torchlight, Jimmy Curran says, bringing you back. He's quoting; he's proud of himself.

—Yeah, you say. I'm in the book. Real Irishmen are, eh, Doyle. There's a Doyle in there of course there is, and a Gallaher, a good long bit on a Gallaher, Ignatius. Lenehan, like Leo. I know a Martin Cunningham, sells web sheet. McHugh, O'Molloy. How many different characters? I wonder. We just saw our Buck Mulligan, with the horn. There's some guy in Canada has done the work; it's at the library. Word count, quarter million. Most common word: *the*. What's the word known to all men? Fuck, maybe *the*.

Your heart sinks and somehow you say, Brownie's dead.

—Brownie lives! Jimmy Curran says excitedly.

You tell him what you know. You square the paper around for the two of them to read.

—Late bull into the night desk. Merchant probably still there with Farragut, Phillies wrap-up. He pulled it, I bet.

Doyle doesn't know him. Curran looks shaken. You offer him your flask. He declines, but you take it for him. Black coffee velvet.

—Did you see him in New York? Doyle. A sore point, New York. Drove cab, saw so much. On Jack Paar once. In the audience, Jack Paar asked you, What do you do? Nothing, all you could some up with. National TV. I'm doing nothing.

You tried. What? Wrong? Swim the Hellespont like Bryon. No guts. You tried.

—This is awful, says Doyle. Three people gone, like that.

Change it up.

—Doyle, what do you hear from the girls?

He knows. Something. Used to date Ginny with you with Cassie Meer. Double date, the Thalia. Cabaret once—Ginny singing, "I'm looking for a few stout-hearted men." Queers loved her. Then the play.

—She got married, guy from Catholic. Big fella. All I remember, met him once, something about Nixon.

That's what you meant but you'd better say, No, Cassie. My once affianced.

—Not a word, but she and Ginny are still bunking, I'd wager. Doyle laughs and twinkles.

Back to Ginny.

—That play killed her, you say. The musical. We all went to see it. Closed in a week. Walter Kerr was no help. I told her, Ginny, this is old. You're better than this. Took her downtown to see Billie with Teddy Wilson. Not what she once was, but Ginny wept. So did I.

January. Or February, '54.

—You know, we had a night, you tell the Jims, looking at your eyes in your coffee.

—I bet she was something, Doyle says to you. Lonely voice.

But you don't mean Billie.

Jim Doyle wants to walk and you don't. It's past three and raining still. He's got his CPO coat.

—Wool, he says. You never feel it. Like a lamb. Stand in the rain all day.

—Irish donkey, you joke.

—Jimmy, come with me. We can hop the work train. I know the guy. O'Toole.

You skip down at Broad and Market underground. O'Toole's there with his big watch. Lets you on the platform in return for a pill and a snort.

You don't know how to get home. Ironic, it's the story of Ulysses. Home, *nostos*, getting back to Ithaca, your wife, your son. But you don't know why you are getting there from here. How here? Why you, only you?

You are suddenly felled. Down on your haunches in the subway, the dark tunnel. Where's Charon, to take you to the other side? You wait in some kind of pain—your head, your eyes, your lungs, they've had enough, and you itch, up and down your torso you could scratch if you could scratch. As you squat there, you reach your hands inside your coat and you do, you do, you do, you do.

Somehow better. Jimmy's asleep already, over near the pay phone. Let someone call; no one's calling.

You are beyond silence down here. Unseen and out of the way and still, just fifteen feet below the skin of the earth, whirring at what, a thousand miles an hour; the earth is 25,000 miles round and goes round in twenty-four hours, about that, about sixteen miles a second, you are speeding.

What you want to say, no audience. Always talking your world, loud, loud. Want sound, to hide in, you sometimes think. Noise. But everything's empty here, waiting for the shovel train. Track maintenance, chug-chug. You should've walked it. McGillicuddy probably stocking the shelves at the state store. A pint for the morrow. Not now. Sit tight; you're sitting tight, squatting, asquat the platform, astride a reservoir of ideas, things tried, and not. Jimmy could sleep all night. You never sleep, even when you do—whirl of lights and sounds incessant, unceasing, which word? Eternal. Music of the spheres—b-flat, a blues key. Neat trick. God's a musician; he's Robert Johnson. Orlovitz in New York said Miles is God. Clifford would know, if he's there yet. He is. Good God! Younger than me. Than I. What have I done?

This'll work, you think. Play it out. Your class a sensation. Dwight Macdonald writes about it. About you. Who was the guy?—Albert Erskine comes knocking. Faulkner. This is what you say now and this is where you get lost. Every single time.

You feel the loneliness in that book. The loneliness of all books in that book. That's what deepens after many goes at it—who notices the first time that Bloom aches for not circumcising his son? Who didn't make it. Betrays his father. Who didn't make it. Happens so quick: Bloom revives Stephen in Nighttown; Private Carr dropped him. Has a vision of his son, who has not died—has now lived on somewhere these eleven years. A little boy looking at him vacantly. Who notices, hundreds of pages apart, that Stephen and Bloom separately notice the same cloud obscuring the same sun? Son, now you get it, fifth read.

You don't need help. It's all there—signature of all things. For you to read. Stephen thinks that. Joyce knows that. But you can show others. That'd be a decent job. Do it. Have you lost that shot? Left Temple, why? Left New York, why? The things you should've done. Left home, left the parish, left Philly. *Philos adelphos.* Loving brother. Really? What brotherly love? You're underground, your choice. On your lonesome.

Then what is it you read. What you read or see in the great books, is what there is in you. That's what they enable. This you know, and you've earned it.

What you see here: The guy in the brown macintosh who haunts Glasnevin is the ghost of Bloom's father, who killed himself. The snatches of the note left to Leopold—in that second drawer at 7 Eccles, he kept it—says he is going to his wife, and she's in Glasnevin, and he's not—buried in Ennis, unconsecrated ground. A terrible fate. What a church. That would kill a son, wouldn't it? Who's the real victim. Would kill a father, too. Don't have ten kids. The math doesn't work, you know, you know. He's half the man for every one he had; you once did the math, do it here, starting at 100 percent, goes to 50 with the first, Patrick; 25 with Terry; 12½, Frank; 6¼, Joe; 3⅛ , Betty; 1⁷⁄₁₆, Helen; then it gets easy— convert the whole fraction, not 1⁷⁄₁₆ but ²³⁄₁₆, then just double the denominator heading out, for every halving: ²³⁄₃₂, Agnes; ²³⁄₆₄, Tom; ²³⁄₁₂₈, Vincent; ²³⁄₂₅₆, you.

You vow that will not be you. All you can do, you will do for your son, sons. Daughters. Starting here. What's over is over. You may never know. One day maybe you will. You were all so lonely. Lost generation, that's what Cassie said. Time to be found. Time to keep. Trust the world; trust the reader of all things. It's in the text scribbled there and here, dark or not. The great text of life. Read it. Teach that. To the children.

There's a little light coming into the sky. Home at last. Jimmy, dear lad, concerned enough, though he hides it, will walk you home, and does. You are silent. He seems refreshed. Maybe you are, too.

—So Bob, I've got the questions. The four. What's the fifth question?

You draw a blank, the Clifford Brown solo running through your head; you keep following it. Your "Night in Tunisia."

—The fifth, he says. To get in the class.

And you remember.

—What's the word known to all men, Jimmy? That's it.

Trick question. You are at your stoop.

—Coming in?

—Nah, Bob. My mother'll be waiting up. I'll think about it. *What's the word* . . . okay. Thanks. That was a good night.

—Go get some sleep, you say. Regards to your mother for me now.

You take a long breath, calming. You find your key and squeak inside, go right to the bathroom one two three, light switch, close the door. In the mirror there, you do not look. You hear a clock ticking. . . . It's your Bulova, your present settling around you like a house. You listen, your heart. You hear Marion say your name. You hear your boy's soft cry. Then Jimmy Curran from below, cinder scrape of his skip on the sidewalk. He exclaims to the street the word—*Love!*—a sparrow of discovery in his voice. Then you grab a look in the glass. Why not. You smile. And flick the light off.

ACKNOWLEDGMENTS

I WOULD LIKE TO THANK Bradford Morrow, Stephen Donadio, and Carolyn Kuebler for early support of this work; agent John Wright for keeping the faith; Erika Goldman and her team at Bellevue Literary Press for believing in this book and making it happen.

I am also grateful for the friendship and support of Kevin Gallagher and Lizanne Gallagher Moretta, whose reading of "Finishing *Ulysses*" was very important to me. My two sons, Joshua and Gabriel, remain central to my telling of any story. I thank them for being. Lastly, I thank my wife and partner and first reader, Rebecca Smith, who continues to ask all the right questions.

BELLEVUE LITERARY PRESS is devoted to publishing
literary fiction and nonfiction at the intersection of
the arts and sciences because we believe that science and the
humanities are natural companions for understanding the human
experience. With each book we publish, our goal is to foster a rich,
interdisciplinary dialogue that will forge new tools for thinking
and engaging with the world.

To support our press and its mission, and for our full catalogue of
published titles, please visit us at blpress.org.

BELLEVUE LITERARY PRESS
New York